"Are you afraid of me, Josh?"

He gasped, seemingly shocked she would think that. "No!"

"Yes, you are," she said, stepping closer.

"Liv, don't do this," he said, backing away.

The nickname cheered her, spurred her on. She wet her lips and asked, "Why?"

"Because you might not like the result."

"The result of what? What are you hinting at, Josh?" She smiled devilishly, sliding her hands on to his shoulders. "Are you planning something?"

"No." His voice was a strangled whisper, and Olivia would have declared him a wimp, except his hands suddenly came around her waist...and he hauled her up against him.

"Actually..." And she noticed that his voice wasn't strangled, or confused, or wary. Every ounce of his masculinity came through. "I *am* planning something. I'm planning this...."

Dear Reader,

What are your New Year's resolutions? I hope one is to relax and escape life's everyday stresses with our fantasy-filled books! Each month, Silhouette Romance presents six soul-stirring stories about falling in love. So even if you haven't gotten around to your other resolutions (hey, spring cleaning is still months away!), curling up with these dreamy stories should be one that's a pure pleasure to keep.

Could you imagine seducing the boss? Well, that's what the heroine of Julianna Morris's *Last Chance for Baby*, the fourth in the madly popular miniseries HAVING THE BOSS'S BABY did. And that's what starts the fun in Susan Meier's *The Boss's Urgent Proposal*—part of our AN OLDER MAN thematic series—when the boss... finally...shows up on his secretary's doorstep.

Looking for a modern-day fairy tale? Then you'll adore Lilian Darcy's *Finding Her Prince*, the third in her CINDERELLA CONSPIRACY series about three sisters finding true love by the stroke of midnight! And delight in DeAnna Talcott's I-need-a-miracle tale, *The Nanny & Her Scrooge*.

With over one hundred books in print, Marie Ferrarella is still whipping up fun, steamy romances, this time with three adorable bambinos on board in *A Triple Threat to Bachelorhood*. Meanwhile, a single mom's secret baby could lead to Texas-size trouble in Linda Goodnight's *For Her Child...*, a fireworks-filled cowboy romance!

So, a thought just occurred: Is it cheating if one of your New Year's resolutions is pure fun? Hmm...I don't think so. So kick back, relax and enjoy. You deserve it!

Happy reading!

Mary-Theresa Hussey

Mary-Theresa Hussey
Senior Editor

Please address questions and book requests to:
Silhouette Reader Service
U.S.: 3010 Walden Ave., P.O. Box 1325, Buffalo, NY 14269
Canadian: P.O. Box 609, Fort Erie, Ont. L2A 5X3

The Boss's
Urgent Proposal

SUSAN MEIER

SILHOUETTE *Romance* ®

Published by Silhouette Books

America's Publisher of Contemporary Romance

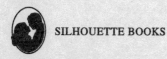

SILHOUETTE BOOKS

ISBN 0-373-19566-4

THE BOSS'S URGENT PROPOSAL

Visit Silhouette at www.eHarlequin.com

Printed in U.S.A.

Books by Susan Meier

SUSAN MEIER

has written category romances for Silhouette Romance and Silhouette Desire. A full-time writer, Susan has also been an employee of a major defense contractor, a columnist for a small newspaper and a division manager of a charitable organization. But her greatest joy in her life has always been her children, who constantly surprise and amaze her. Married for more than twenty years to her wonderful, understanding and gorgeous husband, Michael, Susan cherishes her role as a mother, wife, sister and friend, believing them to be life's real treasures. She not only cherishes those roles as gifts, she tries to convey the beauty and importance of loving relationships in her books. You can visit her Web site susanmeier.com.

Dear Reader,

A few years ago when I attended my first writer's conference, I heard the term "woman in jeopardy" used to describe a book, and I have to admit I was confused. Not by the idea that a woman could find love while facing danger, but because there was no category called "man in jeopardy." I thought that was very sexist.

Then I realized that there were plenty of "men in jeopardy" books. In fact, most romance novels are about men in jeopardy...men who are in danger of never loving again as a result of the pain of a past experience, or men who are in danger of never being able to love at all. They might not lose their physical lives, but it's clear they will never know joy. Some will never know peace.

These heroes intrigue me because they are usually the sweet, sensitive men that most of us long to find, now emotionally closed by a life struggle they couldn't win. Not because they weren't strong, but because that loss was part of their destiny. More than that, though, these men call to me because their pain is real or it wouldn't be debilitating.

In *The Boss's Urgent Proposal* and the two books that will follow, I've taken up the challenge of exploring the lives and loves of three broken heroes, wonderful men struggling to survive a life tragedy and love again. All three suffered an enormous loss, all three go at the challenge of finding love differently, but each will work his way into your heart.

I hope you enjoy their stories.

Susan Meier

Chapter One

"Goodbye, Josh."

For thirty seconds Olivia Brady stood by the door of Josh Anderson's office, hoping the real meaning of her words would sink in, but they didn't. If her boss had caught what she said, he didn't give any thought to the "big picture," only heard what he wanted to hear, or maybe what he expected to hear.

"Goodnight," Josh called, not looking up from the paper he was reading, hardly paying attention to his own mumbled farewell, let alone Olivia's very clear, very distinct, very *permanent* goodbye.

"I have a long drive ahead of me in the morning. So once I pack my car tonight, I'm just going to find a hotel and get right to bed," Olivia said, providing a less-than-subtle clue with her hint about the long drive and praying he would finally grasp what she was telling him. "I said all my other goodbyes last night at my going-away party."

"That's good."

"Yeah, I can't believe I'm doing this," Olivia began, but for the first time since she'd come to his office door, Josh glanced up from the report he was reading. His sharp brown eyes caught her gaze and, as always, Olivia was overwhelmed by how attractive he was. Not only were his eyes clear and direct, but all of his other features were striking and distinct. His nose was straight. His cheekbones were high and angular. His chin was perfect. Thick black hair framed his flawless face and emphasized his dark eyes. The black suit, white shirt and red print tie he wore added to the drama of both his coloring and attractiveness. The only word to describe him was *breathtaking*.

"I'm sorry, Olivia, but I really don't have time to chat tonight. Since Mr. Martin ordered me to come up with a strategy to combat the movement of Bee-Great Groceries into the territory of our food-store chain, I haven't had two minutes of peace. I don't mean to be rude, but I do have to get this work done."

"Yeah, I see that," Olivia said, though tears stung her eyes. "I'm sorry."

"Good. Great. No harm done," Josh said, bending his head to his work again. "I'll see you Monday."

Olivia turned toward his door. "No, you won't," she whispered, then left his office. Forever. For good. She wasn't coming back on Monday.

Not ten minutes after he had finally been left alone, Josh's cousin Gina, director of human resources of Hilton-Cooper-Martin Foods, a grocery store chain owned by her father and his family, came barreling into Josh's office. This time, he didn't bother to hide his irritation.

"Gina, you above everybody else should know that your father will skin me alive if I don't come up with a halfway decent proposal for keeping our market share when Bee-Great is trying everything under the sun to steal it from us.''

Shoving wayward strands of her thick, sable-colored hair off her face, Gina glared at him. ''Josh, you're an idiot. As if it wasn't bad enough that you're so ill-mannered you didn't have twenty seconds to say good-bye to a secretary who's been more loyal to you than you deserve, now you're refusing to help me find someone new!''

''Whoa! Whoa! Slow down,'' Josh said. ''What are you talking about?''

''Don't play stupid, Josh. We thought it was pompous and rude enough that you missed Olivia's going-away party, but I sent you three memos reminding you that she was leaving and that you would have to help me find you another secretary. Olivia might have covered for you last night by telling everybody you were working, but I don't have time for your antics.'' She leaned over his desk and glared at him. ''I need help finding her replacement, and whether you like it or not, you're going to help me.''

As Josh stared at his cousin things began to sink in, and the conclusion he drew threw him into shock. ''Olivia quit?''

''Oh, come on, Josh, I sent you three memos.''

Sweat beaded on his forehead and his chest tightened. *Olivia quit?* He would never get through this assignment without her. ''I swear, I didn't get them.''

Without so much as a cursory glance at his desk, Gina reached for the top documents in his in-box. She handed them to Josh. ''Not only did you get the memos, but it appears Olivia went out of her way to try to make sure you would see them.''

Josh sagged in his seat. "Oh, my gosh. I was just so rude to her."

"I can only imagine."

He sent his cousin a withering look. "I didn't say anything nasty. I just told her I didn't have time to chat. That I'd see her Monday morning."

"You didn't have time to go to her party. You didn't have time to say goodbye. Yeah, you're a dream boss. You make me wish my dad didn't own controlling interest in this company so I could work for someone as wonderful as you."

"There's no need to be facetious, Gina," Josh said, rising from his seat. "I've been very busy. I forgive myself."

"Well, good for you. I'm glad you're emotionally well balanced," she said sarcastically.

But Josh let her comment slide. He *had* been busy, and because it was her father who had overwhelmed him with work, Gina knew it, too. He just wished he would have come up for air long enough to see that his very faithful, very talented, very hard-working secretary was leaving him.

"But that doesn't get you out of finding Olivia's replacement." Gina set a stack of résumés on his desk. "I'll add more to these Monday morning, then I want your recommendations and a calendar of when I can schedule interviews."

"Consider it done," Josh said.

Gina sighed with disgust and strode out of the room, and Josh went back to work. But when he was completely sure she couldn't see him, he slumped over his desk. How had he missed Olivia's resignation? He had been rude. Inconsiderate. He'd failed to attend Olivia's going-away party, for Pete's sake! Sure he had been inundated with work, but deep down inside he knew he owed Olivia an apology. Unfortunately, she was already gone and he wasn't going to get the chance to make one.

Worse, he realized, glancing around at his cluttered desk and the rows of filing cabinets that lined the wall of Olivia's cubicle, there was no way in hell he could train her replacement. Two years ago, she had taken over little things like his minor chitchat correspondence. Only she knew the filing system. Only she knew the names, addresses and phone numbers that he needed and when he needed them.

He was in big trouble!

Of course, if he went to Olivia's house on the pretense of seeking her help to train her replacement, he could also edge in an apology without looking completely desperate. Not only would they both feel better, but also, once he explained that he hadn't understood she was quitting her job, he could probably persuade her to come back for a week or two until they found a replacement and trained him or her.

He was sure he could persuade Olivia. She was a levelheaded, sincere woman, and a good sport. A champ. A woman among women.

And he was also director of marketing and advertising. He knew how to get people to see his point and do his bidding. Combining Olivia's respectful disposition and his skill at illustrating the obvious, he was positive he could have Olivia back on her office chair Monday morning without so much as a ripple of unease.

All Olivia had to do to dry her tears was remember how many times she had covered for her boss, how many times he had taken advantage of her and how many times he had behaved as if she were a convenience, not a person.

As she strode to her car, she didn't even see the celebrated blossoms of spring in Georgia, feel the warmth of the March sun or smell the fresh air that signaled new life. All she could think of was how poorly Josh had treated her, and how foolish she had been to let him.

With every mile she drove on her way to her apartment, huge chunks of grief and sadness dislodged from her soul, but more than that she got angry. Furious. She was so damned glad to be moving on with the rest of her life that she hoped she never saw Josh Anderson again.

She was grateful—thrilled—he had been obnoxious when she tried to say goodbye. It was painful to think she had wasted four years of her life being head over heels in love with the guy. This rude awakening was exactly what she needed to force her to face the truth and assure that she didn't change her mind or have any regrets. After the way he had treated her, she was absolutely certain she wouldn't have to worry about being *nice* to him again, let alone falling back in love with him. Let alone reversing her decision and staying in Georgia one minute beyond her deadline!

When there was a knock at her apartment door only a few minutes after she arrived home, Olivia peered up from the final box she was packing and wondered who the heck it could be. Positive it was a well-wisher, hopefully somebody with takeout dinner, she answered the door with a smile.

When she saw Josh, her smile faded and she said, "What do you want?"

"Hey, is that any way to treat a guy who is here to apologize?"

She only stared at him. It was odd. Now that she had faced the truth about him, and now that he was no longer her boss, she didn't have the butterflies in her stomach that she usually got. They were equals. On even ground. He didn't hold her future in his hands anymore.

Heck, she didn't even *like* him anymore.

She could talk to him any way she wanted.

"I'm going to take a wild stab at this and guess that you're here because Gina finally got you to understand that today was my last day."

Josh shuffled his feet. "Yes and no. Come on, Liv, I've been busy. You know that better than anybody else. And I'm sorry. I'm really, really sorry. I feel like a heel for not realizing you were going."

"They had a cake for me sitting by the coffeepot. You ate three pieces, but didn't see the Good Luck in Florida decoration? You're a marketing whiz who graduated from Princeton. I'm just about certain you can read."

"Come on, Liv," he groaned. "I've been preoccupied. Florida? You're moving to Florida?"

"My mother lives there."

"Oh, so you're moving to be with family?"

She almost told him she was moving to get away from him, but thought the better of it. Not that he didn't deserve it, but she didn't want him to know she had spent the past four years desperately hoping he would notice her, desperately wishing he would fall in love with her. He had embarrassed her enough for one lifetime—or maybe she had embarrassed herself by not waking up sooner. But she was awake now and she wasn't letting her guard down.

"Look, Josh, I'm busy. I've got to pack these things in my car. And then I need to find a hotel and go to bed early so I can be on the road first thing in the morning to avoid some of the traffic."

"What part of Florida?"

"What difference does it make?" Olivia said, getting angry. Now that she wanted him out of her life, it appeared he wanted to camp at her front door.

"I'm just curious. We've been together three years—"

"Four," she interrupted him.

"Four years. Four *long* years," he said, ambling into her living room, which was empty except for boxes. "And now you're just going. It doesn't feel right."

For the first time since his arrival, Olivia began to weaken. He finally got it. Her leaving didn't feel right. It felt forced and awkward.

Still, it was too late.

This time she shuffled her feet. "Yeah, it feels weird."

"And it's the worst possible time for Hilton-Cooper-Martin."

Olivia swallowed. That was the one part she regretted. And her only Achilles' heel. She hadn't intended to leave when all hell was breaking loose for the company that had employed her and paid her generously for four years. But she had set a deadline of one year to get him to notice her, and she had promised herself she would leave if he didn't. In the past twelve months she had tried everything under the sun to get Josh to see her as a woman, to ask her out, or even to hold a more personal conversation with her, but he hadn't. So, keeping the deal she made with herself, she gave up what was clearly an unrequited love and turned in her two-week notice. She had actually resigned before Gina's father, Hilton Martin, gave Josh the assignment that buried him with work. But in spite of the gravity of the situation, she wouldn't let herself take back her resignation. She couldn't. Forcing herself to admit that her life was stagnating and it was time to move on had been difficult enough the first time. She never would be able to do it a second time.

"Sorry."

He caught her gaze and gave her the sweet, sheepish smile that always made her melt. "You could salve your conscience and save my career if you would stay another week and help me train a new person."

She shook her head. "Can't."

"You already have another job?"

She shrugged. "An interview."

"We can reschedule an interview," he said, as if he still had the right to plan her life, and Olivia straightened her shoulders.

"There is no *we,* Josh. This is an interview scheduled between me and a new company—"

"What new company?"

Josh had never been this curious about her life. She knew part of his inquisitiveness stemmed from his natural gift for digging into a situation and finding a way to work it to his advantage. But she also sensed something else. He stood in her empty living room, gazing at her boxes as if they were strange, wonderful things he should explore, and Olivia got the feeling something was wrong. She knew he regretted losing her. She knew he regretted being rude. But the poor guy seemed like he was going to have a stroke or something.

"It's a law office," she mumbled, answering his question.

He looked at her. He really looked at her...and smiled. Olivia genuinely believed it was the first time that he was seeing her as a person, not just an employee.

"You're going to be a legal secretary?"

"That's actually what I trained to be."

His smile grew larger. "No kidding."

She shrugged, keeping her eyes downward because she was weakening. Really, really weakening. She had fallen in love with Josh Anderson because he was a workaholic who wasn't any nicer to himself than he was to the people around him. Olivia knew he needed somebody in his life who would smother him with affection. She had fallen in love with him because underneath all that Princeton business knowledge was a simple, nice guy who took great pleasure in the most common, ordinary things when he finally got around to noticing them. To him everything was special and wonderful, because in an odd way everything was new to him.

"You ever work for a lawyer?" he asked suddenly.

"Yeah. When I first got out of college."

"I hear they're awful."

"I'm sure Ethan McKenzie will be thrilled to hear that," Olivia said with a laugh, referring to Hilton-Cooper-Martin's in-house counsel.

"Hey, Ethan can be a barracuda when he wants to be."

She smiled.

Josh smiled.

"Just give me one week, Olivia."

She shook her head, feeling the weight of her shoulder-length golden blond hair as it shifted around her. "I can't."

Josh tried to argue, but she held her hand up to stop him. "It's not something you can fix. I don't have electricity," she said, then hit the switch to prove it. "I told my landlord I would be out today and I have to be out today. I have to find a hotel room for tonight. Forget about finding a place to stay for an entire week."

"Stay with me," Josh suggested as if it were the most simple, most obvious solution in the world, but heat shivered through Olivia.

Stay with him…at his house… All alone with him when she was weakening toward him again. Oh, that would be wonderful.

"That's not a good idea."

"Why not?" Josh asked innocently.

Unless she wanted to confess the truth, Olivia knew she didn't have an answer for him. He had the perfect argument and his next words proved it.

"I have a huge house. You would have your own bedroom and bathroom. And it would give me a chance to make everything up to you. Every insensitive, inconsiderate thing I've done in the past three…*four* years," he said, correcting himself, "I could replace with something good. I like you, Liv. I feel terrible about the fact that I didn't treat you better. And I want to fix this."

Olivia couldn't help it. She smiled. There was no way he could "fix" what had happened between them unless he married her. For a silly second she wondered how he would react if she told him that, but decided it wouldn't be wise to mention it.

"I hope you're not planning to spend this week trying to convince me to change my mind about leaving, because you can't 'fix' the reasons I'm leaving."

"Okay, so I'll respect your privacy," Josh said quickly. "I won't ask why you're leaving, I won't try to get you to stay. I will keep to the letter of this bargain."

Though she had already begun to weaken, she wavered even more. She did feel guilty about leaving at such a bad time. Not just because Josh was busy, but because everyone was busy. Before Josh was through he would have everybody working, helping to ward off the competition, saving the company from the new grocery store chain that was trying to infringe on their territory. While she, the one person who should have been there to support Josh and to pay back Hilton Martin for all the good things he had done for her, would be hundreds of miles away.

"I'll get Ethan to write up an official agreement if it will make you feel better," Josh coaxed.

But his proposal had exactly the opposite effect. All the girls in the office knew why she was leaving. They had helped her to forge her declaration of independence. They would laugh at her if she came back. Even for a week. Even to help him.

Especially if she came back to help him.

"I can't."

"What do I have to do to change your mind?"

Knowing Josh would see right through a lie and would also see a little too far into the meaning if she told him the truth, Olivia wrapped her arms around herself and turned away from him so he couldn't look at her face.

"I already told everybody I was leaving. They had

a party and a cake. I can't just show up Monday morning.''

"So, don't,'' Josh said in his usual I-can-find-the-answer-to-anything voice. "Train me at night.'' He snapped his fingers. "I know. Train me tomorrow and Sunday. That way if anybody sees you at the office, you can still say you're leaving Monday.''

He had a point. And she did regret deserting him. And she did feel awkward about putting Hilton-Cooper-Martin Foods in a bind when there was so much work to do.

"Okay,'' she said, but the minute the word was out of her mouth she regretted it because Josh gave her his beautiful smile again. And he was looking at her as if he really appreciated what she was doing. And they were about to spend at least a weekend in the same house, probably across the hall from each other. Undoubtedly staring at each other over Cheerios.

Boy, this didn't feel right at all.

If anything, Olivia got the sudden, distinct impression she'd jumped from the frying pan directly into the fire.

Chapter Two

Josh glanced around Olivia's empty living room, desperately wishing she still had a chair, because the second she opened her door he felt he needed to sit. But without furniture in the room, he was forced to stand on legs that didn't seem to want to support him.

Olivia had knocked him for a loop dressed in jeans and a cute little green top. With her blond hair hanging past her shoulder blades instead of pulled back in the usual ponytail or neat chignon, she didn't look at all like a secretary, but a woman. For the first ten seconds he actually felt dizzy and sort of weak-kneed. He would have wisely sat for a bit to give himself time to get his bearings, but she didn't have a darned chair!

"So," he said, trying to sound casual and knowing he was failing. But it didn't matter because he had accomplished the real goal of his mission. She had agreed to help him get organized so he could train her replacement. No matter how silly or how shaky he sounded, the victory was his. And the sooner he got her out of this house and into his, the less chance she would change her mind.

"I appreciate your doing this, Liv," he said, then wondered why he had the sudden inspiration to give her a nickname when he had never used one before. "But, since it's already late, I think we should get going."

Olivia turned to face him and Josh found himself caught in the gaze of her unusual green eyes. They weren't green like grass, or green like moss, but more the color of the ocean. Sort of an aqua. He'd never noticed them before.

"To your house?"

"Well, yeah. We'll get you settled and then maybe we'll even have time for you to give me some background information about your job before we call it a night."

"I guess," Olivia said, but she stammered and stumbled over her words, as if she were having second thoughts about her agreement. Josh nearly panicked until she added, "The thing is, Josh, I have to be out of here tonight. That means I have to have all my boxes out of here."

A rush of relief poured through him. For a minute there, he thought she might have changed her mind. Or, worse, that she was recognizing the layers of complications involved in spending the weekend at his house. After all they were both single, good-looking adults, and in spite of the fact that he was more than ten years older than she, he was suddenly attracted to her. Maybe she had noticed and wasn't sure if it was a good idea to stay overnight with him.... Or maybe after seeing him in another context *she* was feeling an attraction to *him*....

Nah. That was nothing but his over-active imagination traveling into the land of wishful thinking.

"That's simple enough. I'll help you get the rest of these boxes into your car and then you can follow me home. By the way, where's your furniture?"

"I sold it. I'm going to be living with my mother and stepfather until I get on my feet. Once I do, I would rather buy new things than use what I had here, because I want to make a whole new life."

He knew there was significance in that statement. She hadn't said it with any extra inflection, but Josh instinctively knew that selling her furniture or maybe starting over again meant something to her.

"Well," he said, not quite sure why a simple statement would leave him with a hollow feeling in the pit of his stomach. "New furniture is as good a way as any to make a declaration of independence."

She nodded, and her blond hair floated around her like a billowy cloud. In the thin light of the early evening, her complexion was smooth and edged with shadows that gave her a mysterious, sultry countenance, again feeding the notion that he didn't really know this woman at all, and again making him feel tongue-tied and stupid.

He glanced around at her boxes to get his eyes off her. "What do you say we get started?"

"Okay," she agreed, but now her voice sounded uncertain. Almost as if she didn't know how to treat him anymore.

Josh understood that feeling perfectly. He hadn't necessarily missed that his former secretary was an attractive woman, he had just never noticed that she was drop-dead gorgeous. Not that that influenced how he felt about her. He had always liked her. True, he didn't show her any affection. Sometimes he wasn't even really friendly. But he was busy. He was always busy. It wasn't easy to work for family. First, he didn't want to take advantage of the generosity of his uncle. Second, he didn't ever want anyone to accuse him of not pulling his weight. If he worked harder and longer than everyone else, it was because he had to.

And if that meant his personal life suffered, then so be it. The problem was, though, in one ten-minute encounter out of the office, with roles reversed, or perhaps in some respects completely nonexistent, watching Olivia's hair shifting around her every time she moved, and her nice little butt outlined in her jeans, Josh was considering that maybe—just maybe—his life was out of balance.

"Josh?"

"Huh? Oh, I'm sorry," Josh apologized quickly, then hoped she hadn't caught him staring at her, pining for something he couldn't have. Because that was ridiculous. Hormones. An unexpected wash of testosterone. That's all. His goals, his lifestyle, his dedication to a man who had rescued him from a job he hated, couldn't be overturned merely from seeing a pretty girl in jeans that fit as if they were cut to cling to her curves.

"Tell me what box to move and where to take it, and I'll start toting and storing."

"Okay," she said, chipper and happy again.

Josh nearly breathed a sigh of relief. He didn't want to be attracted to her. He didn't want to be attracted to anybody, but he especially didn't want to be attracted to her. She worked for him. Any move he made or inadvertently flirty thing he said could be construed as sexual harassment, but more than that she was vital to his plans right now. He needed her to be his teacher…and maybe his friend. But that was it.

Comfortable that his resolve was in place, he took a quick peek at her to see if the sight of her disrupted his reinforced conviction. When it didn't, he knew he was back to normal. It was for both of their benefit that he didn't see her as anything other than a secretary, and if it killed him over the next few days, he would treat her as impersonally as possible.

They stepped into Josh's foyer a little more than an hour later and Olivia gasped with appreciation. Pale oak trimmed the three-tiered stairway that led to an open second-floor hall. Ceramic tile glistened beneath her feet. A sparkling chandelier hung from a glittery chain.

"Oh, gosh, Josh, your house is fantastic."

"Thank you. I like it," he said, taking her summer-weight jacket when she handed it to him.

"Did you do this yourself?" she asked, peeking around the corner at a comfortable room that was furnished in Southwest American decor. Earthy greens, hazy pinks and muted browns in the accent rug, sofa, and chairs came to life as soon as Josh turned on an overhead light.

"Gina helped. But the truth is I know what I like, and when I see what I like I…" He paused, and his face scrunched with an odd look before he slowly added, "I usually go after it. Not always, though, because some things aren't meant to be. Or aren't meant to happen."

When he said the last, Olivia got the distinct impression he wasn't talking about furniture anymore. For a fleeting second she worried that he had somehow caught on to the fact that she was unreasonably attracted to him and was warning her off, but that couldn't be it. He hadn't in four years figured out she had a crush on him. It was a stretch to think he saw it now. Besides, she hadn't succumbed to his magnetic pull yet. Her resolve was in place. He might be good-looking and sexy, but even if she loved him to pieces, he didn't love her. She was done pining over unrequited love.

But as he led her from the homey living room, through a formal dining room and into a cheerful kitchen decorated with a red-and-white tablecloth, curtains and chair pads, Olivia had second thoughts about her resolution. In fact, being in the room felt downright spooky. All her girlhood she had dreamed of a kitchen exactly like this one, and though she hadn't precisely envisioned the living room, she loved it. She could live in this house as comfortably as he could, and that seemed to point out that they were more alike than they realized and might even be a sign that they were made for each other.

She stopped that conclusion. Immediately. Her decision was final. The man didn't love her. She needed to go. She *was* going. There was a big, wide wonderful world that she had missed while longing for him to notice her. She wasn't missing another minute of it.

"So, is there anybody expecting you in Florida?"

"Oh, my gosh! Yes. My mother," Olivia said. "I need to call her and let her know I won't be arriving tomorrow."

He smiled. "My thought exactly. Why don't you use the phone in the den while I see if I can find something to make for dinner? If I can't find anything, I'll order out for pizza. Anything special you like on your pizza?''

"No. I'm sort of a cheese-and-sauce girl. Nothing fancy for me.''

"You don't even like pepperoni?'' he asked quizzically.

She grimaced. "I don't mean to be difficult, but no. If you don't mind, I hate pepperoni and I hate picking it off even more.''

Josh's expression changed so rapidly, Olivia couldn't follow it. "I hate pepperoni, too.''

They looked into each other's eyes for about thirty seconds, and though Olivia knew she was digesting the significance of yet another thing they had in common, she also knew he was not.

He didn't like her.

He wasn't attracted to her.

Heck, he hardly realized she was a woman. She had to remember that!

"I'm going to go call my mom,'' she said, then turned and fled the room. At least this time, she not only left as she planned, she actually made it away from him without him changing her mind.

She followed a logical path through the downstairs until she found his den. Walls paneled in rough wood greeted her when she opened the door. She walked to the utilitarian computer workstation, turned on a brass lamp and found the multiline phone under a stack of Hilton-Cooper-Martin marketing reports. Even at home the man worked.

Olivia got a tug on her heartstrings. He desperately needed someone to care for him, to bring love into his life, to make his world warm and filled with simple pleasures, and she wanted so much to be that person.

But she also knew she had wasted enough time. Josh didn't want her. If she were truly the woman who could bring joy to his world she would have figured out a way to do it in four years.

"Hello, Mama?" she said, when her mother answered the phone. "It's Olivia."

"Oh, Liv, thank God it's you," her mother said, and though Olivia had heard that nickname a million times it suddenly struck her that only her mother ever used it. But, tonight, Josh had. "When you didn't call from your hotel, we were worried sick that something happened."

"Well, something did happen," Olivia said, leaning back in Josh's office chair and twisting the phone cord around her finger. "Since my job doesn't really interface with anyone else's, and they haven't found a replacement for me yet..."

"Oh, my Lord, you're staying aren't you?" her mother said, sounding discouraged. "Liv, honey, I thought—"

"It's not what you think," Olivia said, interrupting her mother in a rush. "I'm staying the weekend. I'm going to explain my job to Josh and tell him where to find things, so he can train a replacement. We might have to go into the office tomorrow," she said, realizing that unless she actually showed him her filing system Josh would never understand it. "But then I'll be on my way."

"Good. Good," her mother said, her tone indicating that she was trying to be understanding and supportive.

"Mama, don't worry," Olivia said to alleviate her mother's fears. "I've learned my lesson."

"It isn't that I don't think Josh is a nice guy. When I met him at your company picnic, I thought he was a great guy. A very sweet, polite boy who seemed to focus too much on work. But, Liv, you have to start thinking about yourself and you have to stay in the real world. Remember what happened to me?''

Olivia bit back a sigh. "Yes, Mama."

"After your father died I waited ten years for Greg Ruppert to marry me, but he never did. And two weeks after I came to my senses and broke up with him I found the right man. I've not only been happy as a clam since then, I've found peace, and joy, and a purpose in life.''

"I know," Olivia said softly, realizing it was true.

"And I honestly believe your right man is just around the corner," Olivia's mother continued. "I can feel it. I can feel it in my heart and soul in the way only a mother can feel these things. I just know you're about to find your real Prince Charming.''

At that, Olivia smiled. Her mother relied on instincts and what she called lessons from history to make some fairly accurate predictions. If Karen Brady Franklin said she believed with her mother's heart and soul that Olivia was about to meet her Prince Charming, then Olivia also believed it was true. She felt a surge of regret that Josh Anderson wasn't the man of her dreams, but put that feeling down as old habit. She had wanted him to be the man of her dreams for so long, it was hard not to think of him in that context, and she supposed that was really what her mother was worried about. She was afraid that Olivia wouldn't be able to break the ties. And if she didn't she would miss out on her real destiny.

Looking at the big picture of her life, and the four wasted years, Olivia had to agree that was probably true. Even if her Prince Charming was around the corner, if she didn't get away from Josh Anderson, Olivia would never see him.

"Thanks, Mama," Olivia said. "I'll call before I leave."

"Okay, Liv. I love you."

"I love you, too, Mama."

Olivia hung up the phone with the satisfied, warm feeling she always got after talking with her mother. Though Karen Brady Franklin was definitely opinionated and didn't hesitate to give voice to her ideas or render her predictions, she had never been a pushy mother. She listened with warm-cookie sympathy to Olivia's troubles in grade school. She taught Olivia to stand up for herself in middle school. And in high school she taught her to like herself exactly the way she was and to choose the career Olivia wanted, not the one offered by the expert of the moment.

She guided, she didn't dictate. She listened. She led by example. She let Olivia make her own mistakes and then helped her pick up the pieces with a lesson learned. In Olivia's eyes she was the perfect mother. And she was also the reason Olivia wanted to have kids herself. She wanted to give the benefit of the same experience to her own child. Both Olivia and Karen knew that if Karen hadn't waited around for Greg Ruppert, she would have had more children upon whom to lavish love, but because she had waited Olivia didn't have a sibling. Olivia lost out, Karen lost out. One more reason to heed the advice of a woman who had suffered losses waiting for a man who didn't want her.

"So, did you talk to your mother?" Josh asked as Olivia stepped into his spotlessly clean red-and-white kitchen.

"Yeah. You were right. She had been a little worried, but I explained the situation to her and she won't be expecting me or a phone call for a few days.''

''Always good to keep your mother informed,'' Josh said. ''I ordered pizza. It should be here any minute.''

She smiled. He smiled. For Olivia things began to fall comfortably into place. As long as she remembered her mother's life, her mother's warnings, she would get out of this with both her dignity and her sanity.

As they ate, Olivia began to detail her duties, most of which Josh had once performed himself but had forgotten, given that he hadn't had much contact with them in at least two years. She rattled off a list so long, Josh began to get nervous. But when she described her system of filing documents in her computer and also the hard copies in the cabinets that lined the wall beside her cubicle, Josh felt light-headed. This time he couldn't blame the feeling on being unreasonably attracted to Olivia. This time the feeling was overwhelm.

He didn't realize how much work she did and wondered if he wasn't going to have to replace her with two people.

''Wow,'' he said, leaning back on his chair and tossing his paper napkin to the table. ''I'm never going to learn all this stuff in a weekend.''

''Sure you will,'' Olivia said confidently. ''In fact, while I was on the phone with my mother I realized we could make this a lot easier if we just do the training in the office tomorrow. That way I can show you the filing cabinets, show you what's in the drawers, show you the color-coding system for the different grocery stores, show you the document system in the computer.''

Josh heaved a heavy sigh. ''Okay, makes sense.''

"Yeah," Olivia said, then she yawned. "It does."

"I'm sorry. You're tired," Josh said, rising from his chair. "I'm not a very good host. I hardly ever have people over…especially overnight," he said, recognizing he was tripping over his tongue to make sure she knew he didn't have women over often. Actually, he didn't have women over at all. First, he worked too much. Second, if he was going to sleep with someone he usually preferred her turf. He didn't like people invading his sanctuary, yet he had invited Olivia without hesitation or consideration. And he wasn't uncomfortable with her being here.

Puzzled by that notion, Josh led Olivia upstairs. He carried her small suitcase and she brought her overnight bag. He tossed her luggage onto the bed, and then immediately pivoted and left the room, telling Olivia he was going for clean sheets.

He really was going for clean bedclothes, but the truth was he was confused by how intimately he felt about a woman he hardly knew. He wasn't so blind or so foolish as to dismiss four years of working together for eight hours a day as meaningless, but they'd rarely held personal conversations. He hadn't told her his deepest, darkest secrets. She hadn't told him hers. Yet, he felt comfortable letting her into his house. Even reminding himself that he should be more wary if only because of their age difference, he still wasn't getting qualms of conscience or darts of fear.

Josh liked Olivia a lot more than he realized, but more than that, all this ease had to mean that he trusted her. Pushing himself to the limit on the issue, as he stretched to the top shelf for new—he wasn't letting her sleep on old—sheets, he realized he would trust her with his life.

That took away some of the incredulity and replaced it with simple curiosity. The only other person he trusted like this was his uncle, Hilton Martin. He didn't even trust Gina this way.

When he entered the room, Olivia had already stripped the bed of the old linens. The sheets and pillowcases were wadded in a ball on the floor. The blankets and floral comforter lay on the cherry-wood cedar chest at the foot of the bed. She stood with her back to him, staring out the window, waiting for him, and Josh felt a hundred strange sensations. The one that seemed to clamor for more attention than all the rest was an intense desire to kiss her.

Just the thought of kissing her made his lips tingle. All his blood surged to his chest and his heart beat wildly.

He cleared his throat. "Here are the sheets."

She turned with a smile. "Thanks, you can go. I'll get this."

"You sure?" He knew the polite thing to do would be to help her, but red lights and warning signals were flashing in his brain. The polite thing might be to help, but the smart thing would be to run.

Her smile grew. "Of course I'm sure. I've made the bed a hundred times."

He almost asked for whom, as irrational, unwarranted jealousy swept through him. He tried to stop it. He tried to reason it away. In the end, he tossed the linens to the bed and grabbed the fitted sheet and snapped it open.

"Josh, really, I can do this," Olivia protested, but she giggled as if seeing him doing housework appealed to her.

He gritted his teeth. "I'm fine."

"Josh, I want to make the bed and take a shower," she said, then walked over and tried to yank the sheet from his hands. "If you go I can have this done in two minutes."

"What? And with me here, it will take longer?"

"No," she said, but she laughed again. At his stupidity, no doubt, because Josh knew he was acting stupid. But whatever her reason for laughing, Josh recognized he couldn't remember the last time he had heard her laugh. More than that, though, he liked the sound. It warmed him all over.

With that thought, he realized he was staring down at her. She turned her beautiful green-blue eyes up at him, and he noticed that they were standing so close that with one lift of his hand he could be touching her. If he lowered his face just a couple of inches he could be kissing her.

He swallowed.

Two minutes ago he had his first ever thought of kissing her. Now, suddenly, he felt he would die if he didn't.

Chapter Three

When his gaze stayed on her mouth, Olivia realized Josh was going to kiss her and her breath froze in her throat. Her blood tingled through her veins. Her knees weakened. For four long years she had been waiting for this man to kiss her. Now that the moment had arrived, she savored every second of the exquisite torture of anticipation, stunned that her dreams were about to come true.

But when he returned his gaze to hers, she also saw from the look in his eyes that he was confused about why he wanted to kiss her—confused enough that he didn't follow through. He didn't kiss her. He took two paces back and spun away so quickly, Olivia felt a breeze.

"Well, I guess you can handle putting these sheets on by yourself. Good night, Olivia," he said as he bent to grab the old linens from the floor, and nearly sprinted out of the room.

Olivia collapsed on the bed, wondering what the

heck had just happened. He seemed to be seeing her differently, but since he didn't follow through it also confirmed that he was fighting the fact that the way he saw her was changing. Which meant she couldn't let the near miss with kissing cloud how she felt about him or her decision to leave. She might have had twenty seconds of glorious anticipation, but for him that "almost kiss" was nothing more than a fleeting, confusing thought.

If she were a silly woman, she might be insulted that he was rebelling against viewing her as anything other than a loyal employee. But she wasn't a silly woman. She was a realist, on her way to a new life and only detained in her old one because she didn't want to leave any loose ends. It would be horrible if Josh called her for assistance a few weeks after she was gone, on a day when she was homesick, because she might be lonely enough to return. Then she would be right back where she started. She needed to teach him her job, so she could move to Florida knowing they would have no more contact. She wanted to go and not look back.

The next morning, Josh peered over his bowl of cereal at Olivia as she entered the kitchen. Though he had tried to cover his mistake, he wondered if she realized he had considered kissing her the night before. That in and of itself would have made facing her hard enough. But much to his consternation he had dreamed about her while asleep.

The dream, more than the near miss with kissing, was what really made this first encounter difficult, because in his dream Olivia was dressed in something filmy and sexy, close enough to touch, but always eluding him. That was the good part of the dream. The bad part, the part that woke him with shock and a feeling of bewilderment, was that she also told him that she was leaving him because he didn't love her. Which was ridiculous. Completely ridiculous.

Actually it was wishful thinking. Every time they talked last night, first at her apartment, then at his house over pizza, he discovered there was more to like about her beyond her good looks, which were sufficient reason to grovel at her feet in most male circles. He could understand himself wishing she were interested in him. Any normal man would want this woman yearning for his affection. But given that she was leaving, it was fairly obvious that she wasn't longing for his love, so the second half of the dream was pure fantasy.

"Hi, Josh."

Glancing up, Josh swallowed hard. Olivia stood in the kitchen doorway with her voluminous hair pulled into a ponytail and her body encased in cute jeans and a fitted top, both of which were perfectly innocent. But when he looked at her, he imagined her dressed in the red filmy thing from his dream. In his mind's eye, he saw the swell of her breast caressed by what appeared to be see-through chiffon. He saw the curve of her hip shift against the lightweight material. He saw the long length of her legs.

He would have been mortally embarrassed, except Olivia didn't know about the dream and he certainly wasn't going to tell her. Particularly since her chipper greeting proved she wasn't holding that "almost kiss" against him.

"Hi."

"You got any Frosted Flakes?" she asked, ambling into the room like they were best friends who always had sleepovers. As if she wasn't troubled or titillated by the fact that they'd spent the night under the same roof.

"Turntable below the microwave. Bowls are in the cupboard by the sink."

"Thanks." She walked into the room, her ponytail swishing around her.

Josh rubbed his hands across his face as if he was attempting to awaken himself, but, really, he was stifling a groan. It was pretty damned hard to miss the fact that this woman was gorgeous. He blamed her conservative work wardrobe for his not seeing any of this before, but even that excuse only went so far. She never hid her hair, those eyes or that soft-looking skin. He had to have had his head in a cloud. God only knew what else he missed about her in the past four years. But that didn't worry him as much as the fact that he couldn't seem to be in the same room with her without having thoughts that were definitely inappropriate. Some even bordered on downright lusty.

"What time are we going in to the office?" she asked, bringing a bowl to the kitchen table.

Josh leaped out of his seat. "As soon as I shower," he said, and chuckled a little nervously. "That's why I just jumped up like that...I need to go shower."

"Good." She poured Frosted Flakes into the bowl. "You go shower and I'll eat while I catch the morning news."

"Good." He began backing out of the kitchen. "Let me know if anything interesting happened while we were sleeping."

For some reason or another that comment struck her as funny and she started to laugh. Josh took advantage of her preoccupation with giggling to get out of the kitchen, but also to remind himself that that was the kind of relationship they had. Buddies. Friendly co-workers. Gumbas.

Otherwise she would have noticed and reacted to the fact that he was only wearing a robe. Sure, it was a long, commonplace—all right, ugly—robe, but it was only one layer of material. She could have at least tried to peek around in an attempt to see if he wore other clothes beneath it. Instead, she acted as if she wouldn't care if he were stark naked, sitting beside her.

He frowned. Now that he thought about it, that really rubbed him the wrong way. He might be older than she was but he wasn't *unattractive*. Ignoring him shouldn't be so easy. In fact, since she made it look like such a cakewalk, Josh had to wonder if she wasn't somehow faking. Maybe the real deal was that she was attracted to him, but pretending not to be since he had never seemed to be attracted to her?

He knew that was reaching, but the truth was it felt out of balance to be this captivated by her when she didn't even notice his handsomeness, his innate good-ness or his sexuality. Women were always telling him he was handsome, or kind, or sexy.

Surely something about him appealed to her.

He considered the situation in the shower, while pulling on his jeans and sliding into dock shoes, and he decided he needed a test of some kind. He couldn't come right out and ask if she was interested, but he could most certainly hint and see where that led them.

As he locked the house and, with Olivia, walked through the connecting garage, no good opportunity presented itself, and no obvious test popped into his mind. So in the car he asked, "Did you sleep well?" if only because he ultimately concluded that was at least a way to open the door of communication. If she said she hadn't slept well and gave him a flirty little smile, he would know he wasn't crazy.

But she didn't even look at him when she said, "Hmm-hmm."

"No restlessness?" he prodded, telling himself not to be discouraged because his first question was vague. This one would get much better results.

"No."

Hmmm...

"No bad dreams?"

For this she did at least look at him. "Bad dreams?"

"Odd dreams, strange dreams," he said, hoping she would finally get the drift so he didn't have to buy a blackboard and spell it out for her. "Dreams you didn't expect to have?"

"Josh, I've lived by myself for almost five years. I learned not to be afraid of the dark a long time ago."

Okay, that was clear. She hadn't been restless. She had slept well. She didn't have any "dreams." Maybe the person who needed the blackboard lesson was he. The woman wasn't interested.

He pulled his car into his reserved parking space at the Hilton-Cooper-Martin Foods building. She didn't wait for him to come around and open her door, further confirming that she didn't see him as a gentleman friend from whom she expected courtesy, but as a former boss and an acquaintance.

All right. No big deal, he could handle this.

Though Josh had seemed peculiar all morning, when they got into the office building he calmed down, slipping into his work persona as if he had never left it. Olivia, however, started to feel strange. It had been a long time since she had worked on a Saturday and she had forgotten how peaceful and quiet the building was.

"Now, this is weird," she said when they stepped into the elevator to go to his third-floor office.

"Oh, staying at my house where you have never been is perfectly normal, but coming to the office where you've worked every weekday for the past four years is suddenly weird."

"You know what I mean." She punched his arm lightly, and when her knuckles touched his solid flesh, she got another spark of recognition. He was wearing jeans and a T-shirt. She had spent so much time ignoring him in his robe that she continued to pay as little attention as possible to him in the car and hadn't noticed he was dressed casually. And he looked good. Darned good.

"No. I don't know what you mean."

"It's darker than normal, for one," Olivia said, counting things off on her fingers to occupy herself and get her thoughts off his body. Especially off of how approachable and sexy he looked in more comfortable clothes. "And the whole place is quiet when it's usually buzzing with people."

The elevator door opened, they stepped out, and Olivia added, "And that makes it spooky."

"I'll protect you," Josh said, but he rolled his eyes and walked away.

Olivia followed him to his office. He strode inside, flicked the switch for the overhead light and went directly to his desk. He sat on his tall-backed leather chair.

"You're going to have to be the boss here, because I don't know half the stuff you do. So, go ahead. Take the lead."

Olivia stood uncertainly, halfway between her office and his. It was quiet. He looked different. Now their roles were reversed. Everything was off sync.

"If that's how you feel, Josh, you're in the wrong place to learn my job. My job's out there."

"Okay," he said, and bounded out of his seat, as if her every wish was his command, confusing the situation even more.

Steeped in her own bewilderment, Olivia stood frozen in the doorway. Though Josh had reverted to a light tone, and though it had taken her twenty minutes to realize why he had been acting so strangely in the first place, she'd finally figured out what he was getting at in the car, because now she was feeling it, too. In these unusual circumstances they weren't merely seeing each other differently, they were also gathering new information about each other, and those two developments were shifting them out of their comfort zone. He was having trouble relating to her because he was only for the first time seeing her as a woman. And though she'd always known he was a man, a very attractive, very sexy man, she realized that in this situation where the tables were turned, she would be relating to him in a different way, too. Which meant there was a very good possibility she would discover things about him she didn't know.

Even as that piqued her curiosity, it also frightened her. What if he said or did something that made her like him again? No chance. If she could get beyond him begging her to stay, an almost kiss and ignoring his naked legs beneath a robe—while she fought off wondering if he wore anything on beneath—she could survive seeing a new side of his personality or uncovering a few pieces of his past.

"Let's go then." She pointed to her workstation, the cubicle in front of his office, turned and walked toward it. He happily followed her.

"This is my computer."

"I never would have guessed."

"I'm serious, Josh," she said, but she giggled. Now that she was putting all this together, she had to admit this was the first different thing she had picked up on. The real Josh Anderson seemed to make a lot of stupid jokes. Unfortunately, she found most of them funny, which didn't say a lot for the caliber of her sense of humor.

"If you don't pay attention and we don't wade through everything I do, I'm going to leave without you knowing all of my job."

"Okay, I'll be serious, too, because I know our time is limited and I'm going to respect your deadlines."

"Good. Like I said, this is my computer. I have form letters in here for all the routine things you do. Like when you send information to the shareholders."

"And all Hilton's family members' addresses are in there?"

"They're the only shareholders."

"Okay, that's a good thing to know."

"Here's another good thing to know." Olivia walked to the five filing cabinets beside her desk. "The first cabinet contains press releases and anything to do with public relations. The second cabinet holds advertising things. The third cabinet has family information and correspondence...otherwise called shareholder relations. The fourth cabinet is the special projects cabinet. These are hard copies and notes on the projects that you do for Hilton Martin personally. The fifth cabinet is interoffice stuff."

"That's fairly straightforward."

"Well, before you say that, let's open a drawer."

She yanked on the top drawer of the first cabinet and showed him that press releases were broken down by category and filed by year and color-coded by store.

"I can handle that."

She opened the second drawer and showed him that it was full of pictures that were broken down into hanging folders containing photos taken for distribution, advertising purposes, the annual report, and when something unusual or interesting happened. She then pointed out that each group of photos was categorized and color-coded by store. Each store had advertising photos, distribution photos, annual statement photos and general interest photos.

"We have this many pictures of the stores?"

"That's only a one-year sampling."

"We're certainly stuck on ourselves, aren't we?"

"Haven't you ever wondered how and why we always had just the picture you needed when you needed it?"

He caught her gaze. "I thought I was lucky."

Olivia giggled again, but quickly caught herself. "Okay. You thought you were lucky. Very funny."

He shuffled his feet, seeming pleased that he could make her laugh. "I knew we took pictures. I knew we took a lot of pictures. I just didn't know this was how you kept them."

"Now you do."

He nodded. "Now I do."

When she finished explaining the contents of the drawers, Josh stared at her. "You did a lot of my work."

"Yes, I did."

"And do you know what I'm thinking?"

"Not a clue," she said, but inside she was secretly hoping he would offer her a huge raise to stay. She knew it was wrong, but she wished it, anyway, if only because the proposition would be a nice boost for her pride.

"I'm thinking that a regular secretary isn't going to be able to do half this stuff, and at least for the first year or two I better take over some of it again."

Because that was a very good idea, Olivia refused to let herself be disappointed that he hadn't asked her to stay, mostly because she wasn't going to stay. And her ego was fine. Her self-esteem was fine. She didn't need his praise. "Probably."

"Which also means I should get most of these files into my office."

"We can move them now. We're wearing jeans, and after tomorrow I won't be around to help you."

"Okay," he said amicably, but Olivia noticed that he gave her another one of those odd looks he had been giving her since breakfast. With his dark eyes he reminded her of a sad puppy, and Olivia almost panicked, thinking that he was again feeling the sense of loss and was on the verge of asking her to stay. But not for purely professional reasons, as the request would have been a few seconds before when they were talking about how much of his work she did. Those sad puppy eyes turned everything around and made the request personal. Very, very personal. They seemed to be telling her he knew he would miss her.

I don't want to stay. I don't want to stay. I don't want to stay. Olivia repeated the quick litany in her head. Particularly since the only new thing she had learned about him was that he could make stupid jokes.

And that wasn't a basis for everlasting love. Or even changing one's mind.

"Okay," he said again, shaking his head as if to lose the melancholy mood. "But I only have one empty cabinet." He took a handful of files from the first drawer. "So, today we can only move the public relations things. I'll call maintenance before we leave and have them bring up two more cabinets. That way, we can work on this again tomorrow."

Stifling a sigh of relief, Olivia said, "Good idea."

They worked quietly while they carried files into his office and set them on his desk. But when all the folders were in four tall stacks, and he started handing them to her to organize in the cabinet behind his desk, the silence felt awkward.

Reaching for any topic to break the sad, oppressive mood, Olivia said, "You know, Josh, I've never heard the story of how you got your job."

"My uncle Hilton came to my house and told me that he needed me."

"Wow."

"Don't be impressed. He didn't need me, but it took me a year to realize that because I never caught on to all of the coincidences. The real deal was that I was spending the weekend here in Atlanta with my mother…"

"Oh, where did you live?"

"New York. I worked for a big PR firm in New York and I was nuts. I hated the weather and missed the sun. But most of all I missed my family. Apparently my mother had told Hilton, who made up the big story about needing me, and I bit like a hungry bass."

"It's nice that he wanted you to work for him," Olivia said, taking another stack of files from his hands.

"He didn't *need* me, but he did *want* me to work for him. If I had thought for one minute that he had given me the job out of pity I would have quit. But I realized I was worth my salary and I also knew he realized it, too. So, we're good."

"You don't work yourself to death trying to impress him?"

"I'll always be trying to impress him. What I meant was that I know my worth and seek to work to that potential. I don't do it out of fear. How about you?"

"How about me what?"

"Why didn't you go to Florida with your mother when she left originally?"

"She had a new husband and I was anxious for some freedom."

"Ah…" he said, his eyebrows rising speculatively.

"It was nothing naughty. I haven't even had a serious boyfriend."

He was now starting to wonder about that. In four years, she had never talked about a boyfriend…and he had never asked. It had never crossed his mind to ask. Of course, that might have been because it was none of his business.

And it was none of his business now.

"Did you have a happy childhood?"

"The best. I was a very spoiled only child," she said, preoccupied with slapping dust from her hands after replacing the last file.

Watching her shrouded in the beam of sunlight pouring in through his window, Josh observed again how naturally beautiful she was. Even without makeup she could turn heads. And she was well built. In her nondescript jeans and T-shirt she had certainly caught his eye more than once this morning as she reached and bent for files. She was the epitome of every man's fantasy woman.

It shocked him to think he hadn't seen this before, and it didn't seem right that he was paying attention now. He knew that if she saw the way he was looking at her, or realized that he couldn't stop some of the thoughts he was having about her every time he watched her bend, stretch and reach, Olivia would be offended.

To take his eyes off her, Josh looked at the clock. "It's one-thirty!"

"Administrative work looks easy, but it's very time consuming."

"No kidding." He motioned for her to come out from behind his desk. "Let's go to lunch. Where would you like to eat?"

"Anywhere," she said casually, but he shook his head.

"This weekend I'm going to treat you like solid gold because I appreciate this and I also realize I took you for granted."

To his great surprise, Olivia had tears in her eyes. She attempted to blink them away, but they didn't leave. "Thanks."

Josh's breath froze in his lungs again, as those tears and her whispered *thanks* seemed to trip something inside him. His heart swelled with regret for not treating her better, but more than that he felt *it* again. The godawful urge to kiss her. Not that kissing her would be god-awful, but that the urge was almost uncontrollable.

He swallowed hard and turned away from her, because if he continued to look at that angelic face with those gorgeous eyes flooded with tears he knew he would kiss her. And that wasn't right. Not only was she leaving, not only was he too old for her but she was also staying at his house. *Sleeping* there. Kissing her would just open too many uncomfortable doors.

He took her to a very nice, very quiet restaurant that was down-scale enough that the occupants wouldn't mind that he and Olivia were wearing jeans. She made lively conversation about her childhood and being spoiled, and though Josh enjoyed every second, he wondered why he was torturing himself, listening to wonderful stories from a breathtaking woman he couldn't have.

"And my cousin Lydia to this day reminds me that I cried until I got the extra soda."

"That's funny," he said, and though he meant it, he also knew his voice did not convey one iota of humor. His tone was definitely dispirited, almost sad. In fact, he sounded depressed. And why shouldn't he be? He'd just discovered she was funny and cute and liked rigatoni, and she was leaving.

But he didn't wallow in his depression long because it made him mad. He had only once allowed his emotions to lead him, and that had almost ruined his life, which made this sadness ridiculous. Wrong. The woman was leaving to make a better life for herself. To be with family. Hadn't he moved home to be with his family? Yes, he had. So he shouldn't want to stop Olivia.

Finishing his coffee, he vowed to himself that he would get back in line because there was absolutely no way in hell he wanted her to recognize that all his odd behavior meant he was attracted to her. Now that he'd acknowledged his disappointment, he could let it go and do the right thing. He had to treat her as impersonally as he always had.

* * *

In the car, on the return trip from the restaurant, Josh's puzzling behavior started to fall into place for Olivia. She had seen the way he was looking at her the day before. He also seemed to be considering kissing her for the first time. This morning he said he appreciated her. And, at lunch, he was downright attentive.

It seemed he finally realized he liked her.

And she was leaving.

Part of her wanted to scream. The other part was instructing her to shut up and chill. Yes, he might realize he was attracted to her. Yes, he might even recognize they were sort of made for each other. But she couldn't derail her plans based on a bunch of facial expressions and guesses about what he was thinking.

She needed for him to do something substantial, something concrete, before she even considered staying. Still, if he did something to prove that what she suspected was accurate, then she would be a fool to leave just when things were going her way.

But he had to do something. Something solid. Something that couldn't be misinterpreted.

They returned to the building in the same awkward silence they had shared in the car. In the elevator, he asked if she still felt that the dark, quiet office was spooky. She smiled at him and said no. He smiled back. Because that was not concrete, she didn't make too much of it. But she also realized that now she was looking for a sign, the way she had been seeking some kind of sign from him every day for the past four years. Which meant she was behaving the way she had always behaved with him—and that wasn't good.

Telling herself that her inattention might have been what caused him to pay attention, Olivia knew she had to stop thinking about him. She had to treat him indifferently so he could come to his conclusions about her on his own, the way he should come to them.

They walked into his office, and when Olivia saw Josh's cluttered desk she crossed her arms on her chest and frowned. "You know, before I go, it might be a big help to you if we cleared off your desk." She patted the stack of papers in his in-basket for emphasis, and when she lifted her hand a document fell to the floor. Without thinking she bent to pick it up.

"Yes, it would," Josh agreed. His voice sounded forced. As if he were in some kind of physical distress. She peered at him curiously, but he had busied himself with the stack of papers. Olivia frowned. Again, a weird voice did not constitute a confession. Not even of interest. Forget about undying love.

"I'll go get a notebook."

"Good idea."

When she returned they proceeded to sift through the stacks of unattended correspondence, requests for information and typical propaganda. Josh would choose something from the stack and tell her what it was, and Olivia would show him where it was filed, as she filed it. Correspondence that needed a reply was marked with the number of the form letter reply stored in her computer, which she promised to show him the next day. And junk was identified as such and tossed into his trashcan.

She could tell he was amazed by how quickly they had gone through the stack. But when they came to the final item on his desk, a square white envelope that looked like personal stationery, Josh gasped.

"This is an invitation to a party at Hilton's home."

"You should mark it in your book," Olivia said, as

if giving him directions, "then create some kind of reminder so you don't forget to go."

"That's just it. It's tonight."

"Oh. Then you better rent a tux."

"I own one."

"Then you're set."

"Not really," he said, glancing up at her. He held her gaze for several seconds, then he said the words Olivia had yearned to hear for four long years.

"Would you come with me?"

Chapter Four

Considering this the concrete evidence she was seeking, Olivia didn't ask if any other Hilton Martin employees were invited to the party. She didn't care who saw her there. As long as she and Josh were going as a couple, she had won. Finally. Finally, he had asked her out. And she *wanted* her co-workers to see that.

"Yes! Yes! I would love to go to the party."

"Good, because I would feel awful leaving you alone at my house while I attended."

She peered at him. "Excuse me?"

"I said, I would feel awful leaving you at my house alone while I attended, since I basically talked you into staying this weekend and you have nowhere else to go, and no one else to call for entertainment."

Olivia blinked rapidly, trying to shift herself into the actual conversation and out of the one she thought they were having. She seriously wondered if the man had a death wish, because she was as close as she would ever come in her life to strangling someone.

No, she thought, this wasn't his fault. It was hers. She had misinterpreted his invitation. But in her own defense, she had made the mistake because of the way he kept looking at her. The more she pondered the situation, the stolen glances, the inadvertent flirtations, the continual drop of his gaze to her mouth as if he was frequently debating whether or not to kiss her—the more she knew he was attracted to her, but he was being stubborn.

Or he had a good reason for not wanting to get involved with her. Considering the situation objectively she had to admit there was a big gap in their ages. Because it didn't bother her, she had dismissed it immediately, but she suddenly recognized it might bother stuffy Josh. Taking that theory one step further, she realized his being concerned about the difference in their ages actually explained how four years could slip by with him not even noticing she was female. If he would never consider getting involved with someone so much younger, he would never look at her in the context of being a potential lover.

Given Josh's conservative nature that made more sense than to simply think he'd been deaf, dumb and blind to her for four years. But it didn't make her any happier. In the end, she decided it was his prerogative if he didn't want her. However, that didn't mean she had to accept it graciously. Oh, she would be subtle. But if he was rejecting her, she had every right in the world to let him see what he was missing. And if he was simply being obstinate, she had every right in the world to push him so they wouldn't miss out on a good relationship because he was pigheaded.

Which was why she sneaked to her car while he was showering that evening and dug out her red tank dress.

If he liked her, but couldn't say it or didn't know how to make the first move, this dress would open all kinds of doors to help him admit he had feelings for her. Or, if he liked her but doggedly clung to whatever reason he had for not wanting a relationship, this dress would kill him. Either way she pretty much figured she would get satisfaction of one kind or another.

She returned to the house and tiptoed into her guest room. She showered, did her hair, put on extra makeup and slithered into the dress, then waited until she heard Josh pass her door. She counted out the seconds and steps it would take him to get to the stairway, and when she was sure he was almost at the bottom she left her room. The way she figured, he would hear her at the top of the steps, turn to greet her, and his eyes would bug out with surprise.

Peering down at him from the top of the stairway, she watched him turn exactly as she had anticipated. She saw pleased surprise light his eyes, but when his gaze moved from her face to her dress, that expression was quickly replaced by mouth-hanging-open shock.

He looked from her nearly bare shoulders, down her dress-caressed bosom, to her tiny waist, along the line of her trim hips, the whole way down her well revealed legs to her pedicured feet, currently encased in multi-strapped red sandals.

"Holy hell, Olivia, what are you trying to do, start a riot? Give Hilton a heart attack?"

She began walking down the steps. "No, you said it was a cocktail party. This is a cocktail party dress."

He gaped at her. "We're not even going to go there." After a long breath he added, "Does this thing have a jacket?"

She smiled at him and patted his cheek. "I'm

twenty-five. I decide when a dress needs a jacket. Considering the event, I would say a jacket would be overkill.''

''And I would say that without a jacket that dress is going to kill. But if you don't care, I don't, either.'' He turned and walked through the foyer to the kitchen, where they would exit to the garage.

Olivia deflated. How could somebody so brilliant be so thick? Brilliant people were supposed to figure things out before the rest of the world, not miss opportunities.

Unless, as in her second theory about the difference in their ages, he just plain wasn't interested. Well, that was fine. She could deal with his disinterest. She had been dealing with it for years. Except this time, she wasn't going to stand by his side all night to be sure he was amused.

Tonight she was mingling.

As Josh strode up the sidewalk to the front door, Olivia caught his arm.

''Are any Hilton-Cooper-Martin employees going to be here?''

He glanced down at her pretty face, and was so caught by her beauty he almost missed the fact that her green eyes were bright with apprehension.

''Oh, that's right. You don't want anyone to know you stayed behind to help me.''

''No, I don't.''

The way she said it gave Josh a terrible feeling. As if she hated him or couldn't stand the thought of being seen with him. He supposed he didn't blame her. She had told everybody she was leaving. She didn't want them to think he had manipulated her into staying. He understood that. But what he didn't understand was what she was trying to prove with that dress.

Didn't she realize that she was driving him nuts? He knew he had been giving her mixed signals all day. She had to have at least picked up on the fact that he was attracted to her. But she also had to remember their ages and that she was leaving. They couldn't get involved. So it was unfair for her to torture him.

Unless she wasn't intending to torture him? Josh thought, reminding himself that thinking she wore the dress to torment him was a little narcissistic. Her entire goal might be to have a good time and look pretty.

Well, she certainly looked pretty, and he guessed that every unattached male at this party would want to court her, so she would undoubtedly have a good time.

That conclusion did not thrill him. In fact, his jaw hardened. When he said, "Don't worry. There won't be any Hilton-Cooper-Martin people here. This is a celebration for Uncle Hilton's garden club," his words came out a lot harsher than he intended.

"You belong to a garden club?"

"Don't be silly. I don't know an aster from a hole in the ground."

This time she didn't laugh at his ridiculous joke, and Josh felt an acute stab of disappointment. Which, unfortunately, increased his ire. First she teased him with a dress, now she wouldn't laugh at his bad jokes. It was almost as if she were rubbing it in that she didn't like him.

"Then why were you invited?"

He raised an eyebrow. "I'm family."

"Right, Mr. Petuniahead. I keep forgetting you're family."

Now, that was an insult. Considering a comeback,

Josh looked down into her perky, smiling face, and his brain went blank as his mouth became dry. With those gorgeous, green-blue eyes and those pouty lips, now painted red, Olivia was a woman who could stop traffic. He would give every cent in his portfolio for one darned kiss.

One kiss. Would it really be so far out of line for him to kiss her?

No. He didn't believe it would. If only because she didn't really work for him anymore. And nothing would actually come of the kiss so that meant their age difference didn't matter either. He glanced at her lips, then raised his eyes to catch her gaze, and it almost seemed as if she were reading his mind, daring him.

"Josh, Olivia. I thought I heard someone out here. What are you doing just standing there? Haven't you ever heard of a doorbell?"

Josh pivoted to see his uncle Hilton holding his front door open. Dressed in a white tux, because Hilton had a penchant for being different, and looking more like Colonel Sanders than he probably wanted—though he was much taller and much thinner—Hilton was the epitome of a Southern gentleman.

"We were having a disagreement," Josh said.

But Olivia stepped forward and offered her hand to Hilton before Josh could finish his sentence. "I hope you don't mind, Mr. Martin," she said sweetly, using a demure voice that Josh had never heard from her before. "But Josh invited me to come with him tonight because I'm helping to familiarize him with my files. Inviting me to your beautiful home is his way of repaying me."

Josh watched Hilton Cooper Martin, a billionaire, a

negotiator known for making businessmen weep, nearly melt into a puddle at Olivia's feet.

"Of course not. My goodness. I'm not lying or exaggerating when I say that your being here is *my* pleasure."

Then he kissed Olivia's hand. Josh felt his jaw drop again, but he quickly snapped his mouth closed. He objectively instructed himself to get accustomed to this kind of behavior, because he was sure Hilton was only the first of many men who would be tongue-tied and stupid around her tonight.

But when they stepped into Hilton's foyer and it seemed as if every person in the room turned to stare at Olivia, Josh's objectivity, rather than his jaw, dropped. It fell away like a coat being shed in the southern sun. Every muscle in his body tensed, as if he were preparing for the fight of his life.

They entered the huge white living room—specially created for entertaining—and not one person had the decency to glance away.

"Are you sure you don't want my jacket?" Josh whispered in her ear, positive this unabashed staring would be uncomfortable for his shy, conservative secretary.

But she turned and grinned at him. "Are you kidding? Look at the attention I'm getting. If I had known this dress was such a showstopper, I would have worn it last Christmas, when I bought it."

"Can I get you a drink?"

At the sound of the male voice, Josh spun around, irrationally ready to deck the man who didn't even have the common courtesy to wait to see if Josh was Olivia's date. Luckily, he kept his fist in check, because the man was a waiter.

"I don't think we're drinking tonight."

"Josh! This is a party. I'm not missing a minute of this." Olivia turned on her charm to the waiter. "I would love a gin and tonic."

"My pleasure, ma'am."

"My pleasure, ma'am," Josh mocked.

"Josh, if you can't take the heat, get out of the kitchen."

"What's that supposed to mean?"

"It means, shoo! I want to have a good time. And nobody's going to ask me to dance if they think you're my date."

Josh hadn't even realized there was dancing. He was so caught up in guarding Olivia, when it seemed she didn't want guarding, that he had missed the fact that Hilton had the French doors opened to the tile-floored salon.

About forty elegantly dressed people mingled in the living room. Another twenty or so danced to sounds produced by a four-piece band. The female lead singer was scantily dressed. Her saucy black hair curled and swirled around her like a cloak. Her voice was sultry, seductive. Still, every male gaze in the room was locked on Olivia.

Something inside of him, he quickly labeled it a brotherly, protective instinct, didn't think it was wise for her to be let loose in this crowd. But since he knew she didn't want him hovering over her, he also knew he was going to have to come up with something really good to keep her away from these men. The only thing he could think of to stall for time while he deliberated his course of action was to ask her to dance.

"Okay, I'll shoo. But give me the first dance."

Her eyes narrowed as if she were wary of his reason for asking. "All right."

Josh knew not to get persnickety about her curt answer. He led her to the dance floor, but before they made even one motion in the fast dance that had been playing, the sexy female singer shifted into a slow, sultry song. Mellow and bluesy, it was as enticing as a mating call.

Trapped, Josh felt his muscles freeze and his blood heat. He had more than an inkling that this was a big, big mistake, but too proud to admit that, he stepped forward, slid his arm around Olivia's waist and began to dance.

Though he tried to stay detached and not think the thoughts volleying around his head or feel the physical reactions ricocheting through his body, holding her so intimately ruined his resolve. He decided his only salvation would be distracting conversation and he asked, "So, why didn't you ever wear this dress before?"

She looked up at him. The wariness was obvious in her pale eyes. "Lost my nerve."

"Well, that doesn't seem to be a problem tonight."

"This past year I made a lot of emotional strides. I've changed a lot."

That was it, Josh realized, gliding them along the dance floor. That was why he was noticing her more this weekend and reacting to her in a way he never had. She had changed. She had changed a great deal. But he didn't think it had happened overnight. Her metamorphosis had been more of a process that must have culminated with her decision to move to Florida. That was why she appeared so different.

"How old were you when you came to work for me?"

"Twenty-one," she answered, but she wouldn't look at him.

"I was thirty-four then. Wow. That seems like a hundred years ago."

For that, she glanced up and smiled. "I know. You were still wearing that spiky hairdo that made you look like John Travolta with his finger in a light socket."

"Don't remind me."

"Luckily, I talked you out of that."

"Yes. You did."

"And the sans-a-belt slacks."

"They were suit pants."

"They were ugly."

"I suppose," he agreed, realizing his conversation tactic had worked. He no longer felt incredibly jealous or on the verge of arousal. But something stranger was happening. He felt happy, comfortable. Being with Olivia had always been easy. She was one of the sweetest, nicest people he knew. Which was why, when the song ended and Josh noticed at least four guys standing on the sidelines salivating, almost rubbing their hands together with anticipation, Josh knew he couldn't walk away. He couldn't leave Olivia to this pack of wolves. He had to protect her. Whether she wanted him to or not.

He paid no attention to the little voice in his head that reminded him that by not having to see her with other men he was protecting himself more than her. He paid no attention to the fact that dancing with her, being with her, pleased him. As far as he was concerned, he was only doing his duty.

After the fourth dance, Olivia finally realized what was going on. Josh wasn't keeping other men away because he was concerned for her virtue—he was jealous. Joy sprinted through her, along with a devilish streak. If this dress and this party had gotten him to come face-to-face with his feelings, then she had to give him the final push and make him admit he liked her.

"You know, there's a waiter floating around here somewhere with a gin and tonic with my name on it."

"Are you thirsty?"

Olivia smiled at him. His quick and solicitous response made her think her assessment was right on the money. He liked her—at least to some degree. This party was forcing him to acknowledge it. Because here he stood, at her beck and call.

After four years of waiting for this, she was not above enjoying this moment.

"Yes. I'm thirsty. I would love a drink, and I'd also like to go out onto the patio." She paused long enough to smile prettily at him. "If you don't mind?"

"No. No. Of course I don't mind." He glanced around, obviously taking note that two of the more interested guys had not given up on her. "But I think you should come with me while I hunt down the waiter."

She would have argued, if only for the fun of it, but that would be counterproductive. This was the point where she was supposed to be giving him the chance to admit he liked her. Which meant she had to give him reasons to like her, not tease him.

Instead of looking for a waiter, they went directly to the bar, got drinks and made their way outside, where it was a little colder than Olivia had anticipated. If she had been dressed in jeans and a sweatshirt, the cool March night wouldn't have been a problem. Wearing the scrap of material she was calling a dress, Olivia was freezing.

Worse, though, she and Josh weren't the only ones who had the idea of going out to the patio. Three other couples stood staring at the crescent moon. Now she couldn't flirt outrageously with Josh. They might as well go back inside.

"We might as well go back inside."

She glanced at him, confused when she heard her thought coming out of his mouth. "What did you say?"

"I said we might as well go inside."

Now, why would he think that, unless he had been seeking privacy as much as she had? And if he had been seeking privacy, then maybe he did want to kiss her.

She'd be darned if she would give up this opportunity.

"No, I like it out here."

Even as she said the words, one of the three couples turned from the white iron railing surrounding Hilton's stone patio and began walking toward the French doors.

Unfortunately, Olivia also shivered.

"But you're cold."

"Not freezing." That was a lie, but the second couple meandered away from the rail and back into the house. There was one couple left. In thirty seconds, they might be all alone!

"I think shivering constitutes freezing. At least take my jacket."

He set his drink on the patio table, and Olivia did the same as he slipped out of his tuxedo jacket and put it around her shoulders. She immediately felt his warmth, but she could also smell him. It was such an intimate experience that for thirty seconds she stood stunned and silent.

And in that time, the third couple drifted away from the rail and went into the house.

"Well, it looks like we're all alone out here," Josh said nervously, glancing around him as if seeking an escape route.

Though Olivia tried not to, she got angry. "Are you afraid of me?" she asked, not bothering to hide that she was offended.

He gasped, seemingly shocked she would think that. "No!"

"Yes, you are," she said, stepping closer. "You're afraid of me."

"Liv, don't do this," he said, backing away.

The nickname cheered her, spurred her on, when she otherwise might have stopped. She wet her lips and asked, "Why?"

"Because you might not like the result."

"The result of what? What are you hinting at, Josh?" She smiled devilishly, sliding her hands onto his shoulders and stepping as close as she could without actually brushing against him. "Are you planning something?"

"No."

His voice was a strangled whisper, and Olivia would have declared him a wimp and changed her mind about the whole deal, except his hands suddenly came around her waist, and without as much as a warning he hauled her up against him.

Then he said, "Actually," and she noticed that his voice wasn't strangled, confused or wary. Every ounce of his masculinity came through in that one word. "I *am* planning something. I'm planning this,'' he said, then bent his head and kissed her.

The feel of his lips against hers was so overwhelming, Olivia almost fell, but as she slipped he pulled her even more tightly against him. The quick jolt stole her breath and it took her a good five seconds to recover. Then *everything* came into sharp focus. The smoothness of his lips. The taste of his kiss. His scent that surrounded her.

Olivia let her arms slide completely around his neck, and he deepened the kiss as if unable to stop himself. His tongue found its way into her mouth and she nestled closer, almost incapable of believing this was real, but steeped in every second, every sensation. Their tongues caressed gently, then, as if he had gotten his bearings or assurance that she wasn't going to fight him, his lips slanted over hers hotly, hungrily.

Olivia stifled a gasp as wave after wave of shimmering delight enveloped her. Kissing him was better than her wildest dream had ever been. And it was really, finally happening.

And both of their lives would be forever changed because they were crossing lines with leaps and bounds. Beneath his jacket, his hands roamed along her naked back. His mouth made love to hers. And because they would be returning to his home, together, he might expect that they would finish this when they got to his house. He might believe that she wanted to make love with him.

And she wasn't entirely sure she didn't.

But she also wasn't entirely sure she did, either.

Josh pulled away slowly as if reluctant to do so, and for several seconds they only stared into each other's eyes. Olivia's heart beat wildly in her chest. She could feel the heat and hardness of his body still pressed against hers. She could see the passion in his eyes. Her own tingling arousal warmed her blood and froze her brain.

This was a problem. When it came to pragmatic, practical Josh she had never taken her thoughts beyond getting him to admit he liked her. In one kiss they had broken down barriers she had imagined would take weeks to approach, let alone cross. She had expected to have plenty of time to think about making love with him, to consider it, to plan it. She wasn't sure she wanted to be rushed. On the other hand, if she didn't take this chance, she wasn't sure she would get another one.

"I think we better go home," he whispered. "And talk about this."

"Yeah. I think we better."

Chapter Five

"I'll get the car," Josh said, and almost strode away without her, but he realized Hilton had valet parking. He faced her again and smiled sheepishly. "Sorry," he muttered, then shoved his hands in his pockets. "There's a valet. We can go out together."

She stared at him with wide, confused eyes, and he desperately wanted to touch her. To comfort her, he guessed, because he hadn't intended for the kiss to go that far. But he couldn't touch her. Touching her was what had started this whole mess in the first place.

When he realized she was still wearing his jacket, he decided that was a good thing. People might think she was ill, or she had spilled something on her dress, and not question why they were leaving early.

Waiting for his car, with Olivia by his side, looking shell-shocked, Josh recalled the sound of her voice as she taunted him into kissing her and knew he had heard a sort of frustration in it. If he were a wagering man, he might bet that she had worn the slinky red dress to purposely entice him, and wondered again if he hadn't missed something. And if he had, just how long had he been missing it?

The valet arrived, Josh handed Olivia into the passenger side of his Audi, and he rounded the hood and got behind the steering wheel.

Since Olivia didn't seem predisposed to talk, and Josh was caught up in some puzzling thoughts, he didn't say anything as he drove away from Hilton's mansion and along the streets that would take them to his home. He pondered her statement about having purchased the dress the year before and losing her nerve about wearing it, and his lungs felt as if they froze in place when he came to the conclusion that she might have tried to…well…seduce him long before this.

Because it was such a preposterous notion, he refused to believe it. Though, thinking back to company picnics, Christmas parties, weddings of co-workers, celebrations Hilton had had as reward for jobs well done, Josh had to admit that Olivia had been something like his constant companion. He had always assumed that she was as uncomfortable as he was mingling with the four hundred people employed by Hilton-Cooper-Martin. He thought they gravitated together from boredom.

Now he wasn't so sure. What if spending time with him had been her way of trying to get to know him? What if she had flirted with him, but he'd been so obtuse he'd missed it? What if, as he had dreamed, she really was quitting because he didn't love her?

Suddenly, Josh's tie was too tight. Not only would he feel like an enormous heel for missing the obvious, but also it just seemed ridiculous. Too much like wishful thinking.

When they arrived at his home, they both exited his Audi as if nothing were amiss. They walked to the door, entered his kitchen, and handled his jacket like two normal, rational human beings.

Neither had mentioned the kiss yet, and it was making Josh crazy. But Josh decided that was good because he didn't know if he wanted to do anything about liking her or wanting to make love to her. When he took this situation to its logical conclusion, all of it was irrelevant, because she was leaving. So there was almost no point in discussing it.

Except that their kiss had been so passionate his body still ached with longing, and he didn't understand why she had pushed him into kissing her.

"We don't have to do this," Olivia said, breaking the silence.

Josh suppressed the urge to agree with her, because with everything that was rattling around in his head, he knew he wouldn't get a wink of sleep unless they cleared up at least some of this.

"Yeah, I think we do." He motioned for her to join him in the living room. She sat on the pale brown sofa. He took a seat on the chair across from her.

Silence descended like a blanket, and though Josh was desperately seeking answers, his tongue was tied and his brain was mush. He didn't know what to ask first, or the best way to ask so he didn't hurt her or make himself look like a fool.

"I never did drink my gin and tonic."

He wondered about the wisdom of either one of them having alcohol in this precarious situation, but decided that he needed to do something while he at least sorted through his thoughts.

"Would you like a gin and tonic, or would you prefer a glass of wine or brandy, something that will help you sleep?''

Olivia raised her pale green-blue eyes to meet his, and Josh saw a look of fear or maybe despair. Whichever it was, it was so intense, it had her paralyzed.

"Brandy would probably be best."

"Okay," Josh said, trying to do whatever he could to make this easier for her because her fear tugged at his heartstrings. He would think the despair was the result of embarrassment, but that also puzzled him since she had all but goaded him into kissing her. However, as he opened the bottle of brandy and poured her a glass, he realized that might actually be the problem. She wasn't as embarrassed about kissing him as she was that she had pushed him into it, probably to see if they should do anything about this new attraction they seemed to share.

It made so much more sense to believe the kiss was an experiment than to think she had had a crush on him, for God knew how long, that Josh actually relaxed. He handed her the glass of brandy.

But rather than go back to the chair, he chose to sit beside her on the sofa. He didn't want her to think he hated her or that he was even angry. The kiss was an experiment. So what? Neither of them had really been hurt, and, actually, it was the best kiss he'd had in…well, ever! Without any trouble at all he could recall the softness of her mouth, the smoothness of her skin beneath his palm, the press of her body against his. He could also feel his body responding. In fact, just thinking about the kiss had him responding.

He leaped from the sofa. "Let me put on a CD. It's awfully quiet in here."

He spent the time it took to find the remote for the

CD player simply breathing, reminding himself this was Olivia, a woman he wouldn't hurt for all the tea in China. He wasn't supposed to be thinking lusty thoughts about her. He was too old for her.

Taking the remote with him, Josh slowly sat on the sofa and hit the button to activate the CD player. A soft romantic song slowly filtered into the room. He frowned and picked up the remote again to shift CDs, but when the new song began to play, it was worse, softer, more romantic than the first. He tried a third time and again the third song was a love song.

"Sorry about this."

She looked at him. "What?"

"What what?"

"What are you sorry for?"

"The music. I didn't realize I had such a sappy penchant for love songs."

She raised her eyes to meet his gaze. "I think it's kind of cute."

Josh swallowed hard. "I'm not a cute person, Olivia," he said, because he couldn't think of anything else to say, and with an opening like that they could go down a very wrong road again.

"Sure you are."

Staring down at her perfect peaches-and-cream complexion, pretty sea-green eyes and magnificent mouth, Josh froze. Ripples of awareness radiated through him. Not because of how she looked but because of what she had said. Olivia had always given him advice, encouraged him, cheered him on, but as his assistant, his employee. Tonight her comment had a deeper, more special meaning. Tonight everything was personal. And he liked it.

Maybe he liked it too much.

Suddenly Josh rose from the sofa.

"You know what? I'm a lot more tired than I thought, so I'm going to bed. You can stay up if you like. Help yourself to the brandy." He glanced at the traitorous CD player and wondered if he really was so much of a sap that all he listened to were sad love songs. "And feel free to change those CDs."

With that he bounded out of the room and Olivia watched him go without a word. What could she say? All the while she was worried he wanted to prematurely jump into bed with her, he was regretting kissing her, but not because he didn't like her. Just from the way he'd kissed her, she could tell he liked her a lot...or at least was attracted to her. But something stopped him from wanting a relationship. It could be that he'd had a past relationship that had soured him on commitment. He could have a problem with their age difference, which was stupid because they were both adults.

Or maybe he assumed a relationship was pointless because she was leaving, which would be true enough, except one romantic word from him, one concrete promise, would keep her in Georgia. But he didn't know that.

The entire problem boiled down to the fact that they were both nuts. He for being pigheaded and she for hanging around giving him a chance to be pigheaded.

The phone on the end table beside Olivia rang suddenly and she jumped, caught in her thoughts. Because answering the phone had been her job for so long, she instinctively picked up the receiver. "Hello?"

"Olivia?"

"Yes?"

"This is Gina," she said sounding confused.

Olivia almost groaned. She knew exactly why her friend, Josh's cousin and the daughter of Hilton Martin would be confused. Not only had Olivia come to the party with Josh, but now she was answering the phone in his home.

"Before you get to speculating about something that's wrong, I'll tell you I grabbed the phone because Josh has already gone to bed…which means we're not sleeping together."

As expected, Gina laughed. "I didn't think that."

"Good, because we're not. He asked me to stay in Atlanta for a few days to show him my job and I agreed. But the utilities in my apartment had already been turned off and I had nowhere to stay so he's letting me stay here."

"Good."

"We went into work today and we're going in again tomorrow, then I'm on my way to Florida."

"Good."

"I mean it. That's it. There's nothing sinister."

"Olivia, you don't have to explain yourself to me."

Olivia sighed. "I know."

"Then why are you?"

"I don't know," Olivia answered, rubbing her trembling fingers across her forehead.

"Could it be that you wish something was happening?" Gina asked speculatively, but kindly.

"No. After our escapades tonight, I think I'm going to be very happy to get on Interstate 75 and head south."

Olivia could hear the grimace in Gina's voice when she said, "Oh, that doesn't sound good. Want someone to talk to?"

"There's nothing to talk about. Your cousin is nuts.

He's attracted to me. He likes me. He's told me more about himself this weekend than he has in four years.''

"But?"

"But he kissed me and he's sorry, and I just want to get out of here."

"Hang in there, Olivia," Gina said supportively. "Everything will be fine."

"I don't think so," Olivia said, for the first time giving voice to the sadness that enveloped her every time she thought about leaving Josh. "You know, your cousin is a really, really, really nice guy who deserves a little happiness, but it almost seems he's afraid of it."

"He might be," Gina said. "You know his life hasn't exactly been easy."

"No, I didn't know that," Olivia said, surprised because she never would have guessed that a guy who could afford Princeton wouldn't have an easy life...and he certainly never acted as if he'd had a difficult life. "What happened?"

"Well, I think—and my father thinks—that the reason Josh works so hard is because his father deserted the company a few years back."

"Josh's father worked for Hilton-Cooper-Martin?" As she spoke, Olivia glanced down at the bottom shelf of the cabinet that housed the CD player and saw that right beside a picture of Josh and Hilton Martin was a picture of another man, an older, dark-haired, dark-eyed man with Hilton. He could have been Josh's father.

"Yes. He was one of our leasing people," Gina said. "He traveled a lot and fell in love with another woman. And since Josh's mother is my father's sister, when he left my aunt, he left his job, too.

"We were right in the middle of securing three new grocery store leases," Gina continued. "The negotiations were delicate because our competitor was also trying to move into that territory. We wanted a good deal, but we also wanted to beat the competition in. We ended up losing our shirt in the one deal, losing the space altogether in the second deal, and basically doing okay in the other. But not good. The negative results of those leases rippled through my dad's company for ten years."

"Wow."

"And my dad and I think Josh felt responsible for that by association."

"Which is why he never actually applied to work for this company, but waited until your father asked him."

"Exactly," Gina said. She paused, then she added, "It does sound like Josh told you a few personal things."

"Not many," Olivia said immediately so Gina wouldn't get the wrong idea.

"You know, Olivia," Gina began hesitantly. "My dad doesn't want Josh to work this hard. We've always imagined that once he came to terms with the fact that he is himself, and not his father, and that he doesn't have to make up for his father's problems, that he would slack off a bit."

"That could be true."

"If he talked with you about getting his job, maybe the next step is that he might talk about his father."

"And if he talks about his father," Olivia said, frowning in confusion, "then I can casually slide in that he doesn't have to work so hard?"

"No," Gina said, but she laughed. "I don't want

you to play corporate spy. I just want you to know that if he starts talking about his father, maybe the truth is he likes you a lot more than you think.''

''Maybe.''

''And maybe it wouldn't be such a bad idea to hang around for another day or two and give him the time to get to the point where he realizes he likes you enough to let go of some of the past.''

''He doesn't have an old girlfriend who soured him on relationships?''

''Not that I know of. I didn't hear much about his time in New York, but being as close as we are, I assumed he would have told me if his heart had been broken. The truth is he's kind of shy. You're the first woman I know of who has been told the real story of his coming to work for Hilton-Cooper-Martin.''

''So, what you're telling me is that you think there's hope?''

''Yes, I think there's a lot of hope.''

''I don't know,'' Olivia said, gnawing her bottom lip.

''Olivia, I wouldn't be telling you this if I didn't believe it. I don't merely like Josh and think you're the person who could help him be happy, but I also like you. I wouldn't give you advice to hurt you. All I'm asking is that you watch closely, carefully. If he talks about his dad, something he hasn't even talked about with me or with my dad, then there's a lot more to this than you think and it might be foolish for you to ignore it.''

No response.

''Olivia?''

Olivia spun around to see Josh standing in the doorway of his living room. He wore the same robe from the morning before, but pajama bottoms protruded prominently from beneath the robe's hem. The collar of the top was exposed around the robe's open neck, but the pajamas themselves were buttoned to Josh's chin. Even his feet were encased in slippers. Olivia was almost surprised he wasn't wearing a hat and gloves to make sure not one inch of flesh was exposed.

"Who's on the phone?"

"Gina."

"What does she want?"

Olivia looked down at the receiver. Gina had never said why she called. "Why did you call?" she asked curiously.

"To see why Josh had left without saying goodbye."

Olivia relayed the comment to Josh and he strode into the room. "Give me that phone."

Olivia handed it to him and took a step back. "Gina, it's me. We left the party because Olivia spilled a drink on her dress. Didn't you see that she was wearing my jacket? And we're not sleeping together. She stayed in Georgia to help me. Not one word of this had better slip out in gossip."

Though Josh's tone was light and teasing, Olivia made a few observations. First, Josh had promised no one would find out she had stayed—so he was protecting her. Second, he had come up with the lie about his jacket and spilling the drink very easily. Either he had practiced that to save both of their reputations, or he really didn't share much personal information about himself with anyone.

While Olivia drew her conclusions, Josh and Gina had drifted into personal conversation and Josh was now sitting on the sofa. Olivia looked around uneasily. There was no reason for her to stay and plenty of reason for her to leave. She slipped away and quietly walked to her bedroom. While she dressed for bed, she conceded Gina had certainly given her plenty to think about. But she was so tired that after she climbed beneath the covers, she immediately drifted off.

When her alarm awakened her at seven, she didn't even remember falling asleep. But she did remember the things Gina had told her and she felt odd. In all of the four years she had been infatuated with Josh, she had never once considered there was a reason he was a workaholic. A family reason. A debt of honor, so to speak. The knowledge reinforced a lot of Olivia's beliefs about Josh, specifically that he was dedicated, devoted and loyal to Hilton, but now she knew part of that dedication stemmed from family pride. He didn't want to let his uncle down the way his father had let him down.

And though that fit with everything she knew about Josh, somehow recognizing that his life hadn't been easy changed everything in Olivia's head. When she walked into the kitchen for breakfast and saw him seated at the table engrossed in the newspaper and mindlessly shoving cereal into his mouth, she felt as if she were dealing with a stranger.

He wasn't simply her obsessive-compulsive workaholic boss anymore. He was a person, with a family that extended beyond those people Olivia knew and a father who had deserted not just Hilton-Cooper-Martin, but Josh's mother...and Josh.

"Good morning."

He looked up and smiled. "Good morning."

That he could smile after the events of the night before nearly brought tears to Olivia's eyes. She'd dared this poor guy to kiss her, and he had. He'd embarrassed himself and had to explain himself to his family, yet he still said a sunny good morning to her.

She retrieved a box of cereal and bowl from the cupboard and ambled to the table.

"Want part of the paper?"

"Sure," she said, for the first time ever feeling like she was communicating with the real Josh. And for the first time feeling that she didn't know what to say. Not because he'd kissed her, but because she had never bothered to consider that he might have had troubles.

Looking at his dark head bent over the newspaper, Olivia knew why. He was young, handsome, educated and successful. No one thought he had a problem. Heck, he was related to the guy who owned the company and would some day be on the board of directors, if not one of the people in line to replace Hilton as the company's leader when he retired.

It was no wonder no one ever considered he might have had a difficult past. It was no wonder women swooned over him and men envied him. He seemed to have everything.

And right at this moment, confronted with reality, Olivia had to question her own motives. Was she so shallow that she simply had a crush on him because he made life look easy, and she very happily would have shared everything he had?

"Well, I guess I better go upstairs and get dressed," Josh said, shoving his chair away from the table.

"Okay." Studying him, Olivia felt confused. Did she love him…? Would she love him—*could* she love him—as a normal guy, with a normal life and maybe even a couple of problems?

Chapter Six

Again, the drive to the office was quiet. Olivia couldn't say the reason for Josh's silence. She only knew she wasn't talking because she had a lot of serious thinking to do.

On the one hand, she realized she had nothing but a crush on Josh. Once she moved to Florida that dose of truth would squelch any longing to return to him because she now knew there was nothing to return to. Even her infatuation had lost its punch. Josh wasn't the fantasy man she'd created in her dreams.

Recognizing all that gave her a sense that she could move on. Right now—today—she could get on with the rest of her life with no more worry that she would be miserable.

On the other hand, being with Josh twenty-four hours a day and genuinely getting to know him wasn't exactly unpleasant. In fact, she was having fun. More fun in his real world than she ever had in her fantasies. If she looked at this objectively, spending so much time with Josh hadn't merely demonstrated that she only had a crush on him, it also had proved that he was a man worth knowing, somebody she could truly love in the future.

Then there was the matter of that kiss. Just the thought of it sent a shiver through her. He'd weakened her knees. He'd stolen her breath. He'd caused her to quiver with longing. If he made love with half the finesse and passion that he kissed with, marrying him would be heaven.

And that, she concluded, was the point of intersection between her fantasy and reality. And the reason she didn't want to leave. For as much as she acknowledged that heading for Florida now was sensible, she also knew she would be taking off just when things got interesting. She wanted to stick it out and see what happened next. She didn't want to run like a coward. Because for as much as Josh's reaction to their kiss led her to believe he didn't want to have feelings for her, the very fact that he kissed her proved he did.

With all those tidbits racing around in her thoughts, refusing to let her draw the comfortable, easy conclusion to leave, Olivia was glad to finally get to the Hilton-Cooper-Martin Foods building.

As she and Josh rode in the elevator they talked about transferring some more files into Josh's office, and Olivia forced her attention on Josh's suggestions. She didn't want to dwell on the question of staying or going. She suspected dwelling on it wouldn't help make her decision, anyway. She needed to occupy her brain with something, and though tedious and mundane, file folders and job training took her mind off the tug-of-war going on in her head.

"What's on the agenda for this morning?" he asked as he flipped on the overhead light for his office.

Though he had already indicated they should move more files, Olivia knew it was more important for him to at least review the aspects of her job they hadn't yet discussed. "I think we should start with the form letters. They're numbered," she explained, removing the cardigan of her baby-blue sweater set and draping it over the back of her chair. "I have a list of what letter is saved under what number. Beside each number is the reason you send the letter."

After taking the seat in front of her desk, Olivia turned on her computer. She typed in her access codes and the general icon screen came into view. She activated the word-processing software and immediately opened the file containing the numbered form letters.

Josh leaned on the corner of her desk. His knees were so close she could have bumped them with her elbow.

"Letter number one," she said, producing it on the monitor, ignoring the sizzle of awareness that skittered along her skin at being this close, "is our generic letter that forwards press releases to the newspapers in the twenty-six cities in which we have stores."

"I thought we faxed those."

"We do, but we do it with a cover letter."

He nodded his approval. "That's very professional."

Olivia glanced at him. "You're very professional," she said, because it was true. Even wearing jeans and a shirt, he looked like a young executive. He wasn't the ruffled, rumpled kind. He was always neat, trim, tidy. So was his work.

He laughed. "It seems to me that it's you who makes me look professional."

"That was my job," Olivia said briskly, not about to argue with him since that meant she would have to explain that she'd made the observation because she was noticing everything about him today and processing it through a more realistic filter. Tall, dark and handsome Josh Anderson had been replaced by tall, dark, handsome and *real* Josh Anderson. A flesh-and-blood man. He told stupid jokes that made her laugh. He liked Frosted Flakes and didn't eat pepperoni on his pizza. She was fairly certain he didn't normally wear pajamas because he looked uncomfortable in the pair he had put on the night before. He had a very tacky robe. He drove with fierce concentration. And she'd kissed him. She had kissed him hard. And he had kissed her back.

She turned away from him because all that processing was generating odd feelings. Shivery feelings.

"Anyway, rather than go through every letter, right here and right now, I thought I would print out the list of letters available, along with a copy of each one. We could put them in a three-hole binder and you could reference them as you need them."

"Great idea."

"Yeah," Olivia agreed, the bulk of her attention on the pull-down menus and dialogue boxes that would allow her to produce all forty letters and the list. Her printer began to hum, the first letter came out, and Olivia rose.

"That's that. We can review the letters individually, when all the hard copies are done."

"Okay," Josh said, smiling again. "Now what?"

It wasn't what he said, but how he said it that got to her. He had a deep, masculine voice, which she had always known, but it had never had this kind of effect on her before.

To get her attention off him, Olivia glanced into his office. She could see that the two new cabinets he requested the day before had been placed behind his desk, and she said, "Let's move those files you were talking about earlier."

Even though she had stopped staring at him, she couldn't stop thinking about him. She wondered how long ago his father had worked for Hilton Martin. She wondered how old Josh was when his father quit. She wondered how often he had seen him or if his father had moved away and never came back. She wondered what Josh had been like in high school and college. For the first time ever she wondered if he'd had girl-friends.

He had to have. Even in the four years they'd worked together, he had to have had at least one rela-tionship. If not hundreds...well, tens, anyway. He was too handsome not to have been pursued. And too nor-mal not to pursue someone himself.

He didn't seem to see her confusion, or all the ques-tions she was sure must have shown in her expression. Or, if he did, he didn't want to address them. He said, "Moving those files is a good idea." Then, without another word, he led her to the cabinet and started re-moving files. She followed suit, mimicking the same system that they had used the day before. Each carried an armload of files to his desk and stacked them in the center for refiling.

She took her second batch in as he was walking out of the office. They passed midway and he smiled. She smiled back. Except this time, she knew he wasn't seeing a secretary in the same way bosses frequently see all office fixtures. Today, he was seeing *her*.

She walked out. He walked in. Same meeting point. Same smile. And Olivia had the strange sensation that this was some kind of acclimation ritual. They had spent four years working together but really hadn't gotten to know each other, so for this twenty minutes they would spend walking back and forth, passing, smiling, they were adjusting to the fact that they knew each other in a different way now.

Which was good. Exactly what they needed.

When all the folders were on Josh's desk, he took the position beside the first empty cabinet and told Olivia which files he wanted. She rummaged for them and handed them to him. He caught her gaze, smiled, and said "Thanks." Then he turned to put them away.

After another three times of that procedure, Olivia had the solid sense that they were over the awkward hurdle. They were again comfortable with each other in spite of last night's kiss. But though Josh didn't know it, Olivia had also quickly acclimated to the fact that she no longer had him on a pedestal. Things had not returned to the original normal environment to which they were accustomed, but as far as Olivia was concerned, they had hit a new level of relating to each other. They were real, live people to each other now.

Waiting for Josh to call out another set of files, Olivia let her gaze roam around his office, seeking things she hadn't appreciated before. She had seen everything, even the same picture of Hilton and the man Olivia assumed to be Josh's father he had at his house. But she had never considered the significance.

"That's your mother, right?" she asked, hardly even realizing she was talking.

He glanced at her. "Yeah."

"Does she live in Atlanta?"

"In spite of three divorces she's not only stayed in Atlanta, she's managed to keep the same house."

Olivia's eyes widened with shock. "Wow! Three divorces."

"Yep. And looks like her fourth marriage isn't going to survive, either."

"I'm sorry."

"Don't be. She's not. She could marry and divorce every year and it wouldn't faze her."

Though Josh's tone was casual, Olivia thought she heard an inkling of disappointment or upset weaving through it. "Is that why you don't see her much now?"

"I actually see her a lot." He paused, peered at her again. "Why did you think I didn't?"

Not believing it appropriate to reveal that she'd tried to analyze his tone, she shrugged. "I don't know."

"You think all I do is work."

Olivia laughed. "Because it's true."

"To a degree."

"What else do you do?" Olivia asked, sliding her hip onto his desk as he familiarized himself with the files he had just organized. Though it wasn't good that he had such unstable parents, it did explain Josh's own tendency toward self-discipline. "You've got muscles in your arms that you don't get from sitting behind a desk." She crossed her legs and casually began to swing the top one. "Do you play tennis, racquetball?"

He shrugged, still concentrating on the files. "I golf."

"Golf doesn't give you muscles."

When he turned and smiled at her, Olivia knew he

had only said that to make her laugh, so she laughed. She let her giggle burst forth the way it had wanted to.

"You have an off sense of humor," she said through her laughter.

"I wouldn't talk. You're the one who laughs at my jokes."

"Touché," Olivia said, but she didn't let the original subject drop because she craved every detail about him. "Aren't you going to tell me how you stay fit?"

"I swim."

"Oh." She had never thought of that.

"And play ball. Football and softball with friends."

"Oh."

"I used to run, but that's hard on the knees."

She stared at him. "You do all this on top of working yourself silly? When do you find the time?"

"I'm not married," he said, his attention riveted on the files he was stuffing into the drawer. "I have a lot of empty time."

"It almost looks like you work into the wee hours of the morning so you can play softball in the afternoon."

"Something like that."

"Interesting."

"What about you?" He caught her gaze. "Do you have any hobbies?"

"I cook. I crochet. I love aerobics," she said, recognizing turnabout was fair play. "I visit my mother so I can spend time at the beach. And right now I feel like I'm a contestant on the *Dating Game*."

For that he stopped working and laughed with glee. "You, too?"

She nodded. "Me, too."

"So what are we doing?"

"I don't know. I think because we kissed last night we feel we have to at least sort through this and see if we're missing out on something."

He conceded that with a nod. "That's it in a nutshell."

"But I also think we both realize that I'm planning to leave," Olivia said, giving voice to the other side of the argument in her head, if only because it was the fair thing to do. "So we both know we need to be very cautious about getting involved, because if we get involved, and I decide to stay, but it fizzles, then we're going to have a mess on our hands."

"Exactly," Josh said, not looking at her but intently focused on the files as if she had hit a nerve.

Deciding that they had shared their real feelings about the situation, and they agreed, but neither was ready to make any real declarations or decisions, Olivia changed the subject. "Do you play in a softball league?"

"No. Just pickup games with friends."

"And you see a lot of your mother."

"Dinner every Sunday afternoon." He faced her. "Oops. I better call her," he said, then he paused awkwardly. "Do you want to go to dinner at my mother's, or should I just phone and tell her not to expect me?"

With the fragile understanding they had just shared, it would be incredibly stupid to meet his mother right now. "Why don't we pass on that and go someplace for lunch when we're at our next stopping point."

She watched relief come to his face, though he quickly hid it. "Good. I'll call."

"And I'll go out to my desk and work on printing out samples of some of my other things."

"Okay," he said.

He sat down and picked up the receiver of his phone as Olivia walked out of his office. When she got to her computer, she created hard copies of his weekly and monthly reports, so that Josh would have them to show a new secretary the format he preferred. By the time she was done, he was off the phone.

"My mother said to tell you thanks for staying around to help me."

Because it was a pleasant surprise, and maybe even a good omen, that he had discussed her with his mother, she smiled. "Well, she's welcome. I truly didn't want to leave you in a bind."

"I would have deserved it, since I didn't pay any attention when everybody was telling me you were quitting."

"You were busy."

He sighed. "I know."

Realizing they had beaten him enough for that, Olivia showed him the reports. When they arrived at a natural stopping point, they decided to go to lunch. They chose the same restaurant where they had eaten the day before and returned to the office like two friends. Which pleased Olivia even more. Not only had they come to terms with that kiss, but they were proving that they were capable of an honest relationship. Demonstrating that they could be friends was a very good first step to establishing that they could be more than friends.

"So, what do we do now?"

"Now we should go over those form letters. I have an old binder here," she said, reaching for it. "Since I used paper already three-hole-punched, all we gotta do is slide them in."

"Okay. We're really cooking here now, right?"

"Yes, we are," she agreed, because it seemed like he was getting nervous. They had only about four more hours of working time. Four more hours of being together. Unless she found a good reason to stay, she had no recourse but to leave. Which meant these might be the last hours she would spend with him. Because no matter how attractive he was, or how close he was to admitting he liked her, she didn't really know him enough to make the choice to stay.

Plus, she couldn't discount the merits of the other side of the argument in her head. Recognizing she only had a crush on Josh, and not actually being involved with him, freed her. She had reached the perfect time and the perfect way to leave without regret or remorse.

She started sliding the form letters onto the rings of the binder. "You know, Josh, if you hire somebody with experience, I don't think you'll have too much to worry about."

"You don't?"

"No." With all the letters inside, Olivia snapped the binder closed. "A reasonably intelligent person with organizational skills will pick up on my systems in a snap."

Josh began walking into his office. "Good."

Olivia followed him. "For somebody like you, with a responsible position in the company and who requires a good bit of help from his assistant, five years of experience is about the least I would accept."

"Should I try to find somebody with experience in PR or advertising?" he asked, taking the seat behind his desk.

"I was a legal secretary." She sat on the chair in front of his desk, the chair on which she had sat for dictation, instruction and company news for four years.

The chair she would never sit on again. For as logical as her arguments were to leave, a sense of pure sadness enveloped her.

"That's right."

"Okay," Olivia said, refusing to let her melancholy seep into her voice, then opened the binder. She set it on the desk, facing Josh, since she knew the letters like the back of her hand, and he was the one who needed to know them now. "There are a lot of thank-you-for-your-interest letters, but there are also some generic form letters we send out to people who have complaints."

Josh looked up at her. "This one says it's forwarding a fifty dollar gift certificate."

"Sometimes we do that if a customer has had a particularly difficult time with something." She pursed her lips to keep from laughing. "You came up with this idea."

"I did?"

She nodded. "Right after I came on board."

"Has it worked?"

"It's a wonderful way to win goodwill."

"Well, bully for me."

"Exactly," Olivia agreed, and went through another eight to ten letters. But when she came to a letter that had several blanks that would require his new secretary to input information, she rose and rounded his desk so they could both read the document.

She bent down over the binder, leaning in to instruct him on the data required for each space. Then she smelled his cologne and saw they were less than two inches away from each other, and every atom of her being seemed to freeze.

Josh turned his head to look at her, magnifying the

closeness. Gravity encouraged her to lean forward—two inches, and she could be kissing him—but she fought it. She couldn't kiss him. Though she wanted to. She desperately wanted to kiss him.

But she couldn't. They had put their cards on the table. They knew the consequences. If they started a relationship and it fizzled, it would be a difficult situation. But more than that, she had reached the perfect time to leave. If she went to Florida now, she would have pleasant memories and a new life. No regrets.

He stared into her eyes for a few more seconds, and she wondered why he just didn't look away. If he didn't want this, all he had to do was avert his eyes and go back to talking about the form letter in front of them. Instead, he swallowed hard and his gaze fell to her mouth, as if the decision was the hardest he had ever made, but in the end, he turned away.

Olivia almost collapsed. And she didn't know if it was from relief or disappointment. One kiss from him might have revived her arguments to stay, because it would have proved he was interested in giving this a shot. But though she longingly saw the potential of this relationship, she also didn't want to miss the opportunity to leave without regret. There was no guarantee a relationship between them would work, and she knew if she kissed him again, if they gave a relationship a chance and it failed, she would get hurt, and when she left it wouldn't be with optimism and enthusiasm. She would leave miserable. Saddened to the point that it might take her months to recover.

But the "almost kiss" created a thick tension between them. No matter how sure she was that leaving was the right choice, it didn't stop the growing awareness that they were attracted to each other, but chose to do nothing about it. Though Olivia used the rest of the afternoon to teach him as much as she could, partly in an effort to help him and partly because she was trying to push them through the strain, it didn't seem to work. Several times she caught him staring at her, and she knew that in the same way she was discovering new things about him, he was seeing new things about her.

She couldn't tell if he was debating the same issues she was, or if he was regretting that he only now realized they had an incredible attraction. She only knew that they shouldn't do anything about what they were seeing and feeling, unless they were awful darned sure it was the right thing.

Again, they rode to Josh's house in complete silence. He didn't have a clue what Olivia was thinking, but he did know his own thoughts were a complete mess. Their conversations that day made him believe she didn't give one whit of a thought to their age difference and that once he processed that, once he acclimated to the fact that without an age difference everything between them changed, suddenly he wasn't seeing Olivia as his secretary anymore. She was a person. A nice person. A very nice, very sweet woman to whom he was attracted. And he recognized that he not only regularly took advantage of her intelligence and good nature, he also knew he had conned her into staying this weekend for his own selfish reasons. He could forgive himself because he had needed this help, but the minute he factored in the growing attraction between them, he knew it would be wrong to ask her to stay another day.

Though she could because her interview wasn't until Tuesday and she *should* because he didn't want her

driving to Florida on a Sunday night. Especially since
it was now raining. But if he asked her to stay, the
request could be construed as abusing their newfound
feelings. Unfortunately, if he didn't ask her to stay, he
wouldn't get a chance to explore these feelings. The
whole situation was a mess.

Confused, he unlocked the door that led from the
garage into his kitchen. Outside the rain was coming
down in sheets. Lightning and thunder had been added
to the fray.

"You want to put on something dry before we make
dinner?" Josh asked, knowing that was about as close
as he could come to asking her to stay, or at least delay
her trip, without giving her the sense that he wanted
her to stay longer to help him. He did want her to help
him. He wished she would. But he wouldn't take advantage of her. And he didn't want her to think he only
wanted her to stay because of work. He really wanted
her to stay because he was going to miss her. But he
couldn't tell her that yet. It was premature.

"Actually," she said, then shuffled her foot. "I think
I ought to get going."

"Olivia, it's raining. *Really* raining," he said, em-
phasizing that because he wanted to be clear that he
was concerned for her safety, and not trying to manip-
ulate her. "Stay for dinner. See if it slows down. With
the way it's pouring out there, you're not going to
make much headway driving through the storm. Why
not wait it out?"

As if stalling for time while she deliberated, she
licked her lips and Josh suppressed a groan. He had
never been so torn about anybody in his whole life.
Half of him just wanted to grab her and beg her not to
leave. The other half knew he couldn't make that kind

of request after two days of getting to know each other. Particularly since she had plans. He couldn't ask her to disrupt her life for something that might or might not work....

But it was tempting. It was so damned tempting.

"Okay, I'll stay through dinner."

Josh breathed a sigh of relief. "Great! What do you want to eat? I'll be Chef Pierre tonight."

"You cook?"

"Enough to get by. I can make eggs, bacon, home fries, spaghetti with sauce from a jar, Chinese food from a bag, and anything frozen."

She looked at him. "I think I'd fare better at a truck stop."

"You won't say that after you've tasted my eggs, bacon and home fries."

She stripped off her damp outer sweater and Josh's eyes were immediately drawn to look at her breasts. He didn't want them to go there. They went of their own volition. He had already discovered so many new and wonderful things about her that he knew fantasizing about her would keep him up nights long after she was gone. He didn't need any more vivid images. But he couldn't seem to stop himself.

"What can I do to help?"

"The two time-consuming jobs are microwaving the bacon and peeling the potatoes. Your choice."

"I'll microwave the bacon."

"Good. I love the feeling of a dry potato," he said sarcastically.

She shivered as if that gave her the willies. "Oh, stop. I hate to touch dry things like dirt and flour," she said, looking at him for confirmation because it appeared that was another thing they had in common.

"Guilty as charged," he said, then walked to the cupboard for a knife and to pull out the potatoes. "That's why I rinse before I peel. The bacon's in the freezer."

Working amicably, they managed to cook their dinner quickly and with ease. While they ate, they talked about her first days on the job. In the living room, sharing brandy and sitting in front of his gas fireplace—which Josh discovered really was every bit as good as a real log fire—they talked about his feelings of apprehension when he first started his job. He thought about telling her about his father, but in the end couldn't work up the nerve. But the very fact that he almost told her made him realize how close he felt to this woman. He also knew that since she was curled up on his sofa, sipping brandy, she had no intention of leaving him that night.

"I was thinking that since my interview isn't until Tuesday afternoon, I could actually hang around one more day and maybe come into work with you tomorrow night and review the résumés Gina gave you."

"That's a great idea," he said, but right now his thoughts weren't on replacing her. Or even on her working for him. His thoughts had lodged on how perfect she was, how soft she looked, and how easy it was to talk to her.

"I think I'm the best person to pick my replacement since I more or less know the level of skill and ability needed to do the things I've done."

He watched the firelight play against her skin and smiled. He didn't even bother to stop his hand when it wanted to tuck a wayward strand of hair behind her ear, away from her face. So he could more clearly see the way the heat was pinkening her cheeks. "You're probably right."

"Of course I'm right," she said, but her voice was a soft, tempting whisper. The force of gravity drew him to her, even as she stretched toward him.

"I've always known that."

Their faces were only a fraction of an inch away and he saw the corners of her mouth tilt upward when she said, "Really?"

"Yeah."

"Then why didn't you ever say that?"

He combed his fingers through her long yellow hair. "I thought I had."

"You hadn't."

"I'm saying it now."

He thought those were excellent words to end the conversation, and when his head tilted forward and hers tilted back, ready for him to kiss her, he also knew she agreed. He was saying it now.

He was saying everything now.

Chapter Seven

He closed his mouth over hers, and Olivia felt a hundred sensations at once. The smooth silk of his lips. The hardness of his body. The tingle of the scent of his aftershave. But beyond the physical things, she felt the rightness of what they were doing and finally comprehended what her intuition had been leading her to that morning. A real relationship with Josh Anderson was a hundred times better than the fantasy. And that was a damned good reason to stay.

The kiss seemed to go on and on as if he were memorizing all the feelings they had both been missing for four long years. When he nudged her lips open with his tongue, she gingerly accommodated him. With the simplest act, shivery responses ricocheted through her and her arms slid around his neck, her body edged closer of its own volition, and a soft sound issued from her throat.

The little moan seemed to release something in him and he not only deepened the kiss, he also began to slide them both down on the sofa. Warm delight sprinted through Olivia at the feeling of his entire body pressed along the length of hers. She didn't mind when his hands began to roam, seeking exposed skin. First, because the skin he found was on her arms. Safe territory. But also because she was eager for his touch. Eager to take them to the next level.

He did. Slowly, as if needing to be very careful, and all the while still kissing her, Josh allowed his hand to meander to the underside of her breast. His fingers crept beneath her lacy bra, creating an opening for his hand.

Heat and need thundered through Olivia. Her breath lodged in her throat and she couldn't move. She wasn't even sure she was kissing Josh back anymore until she heard the soft noise of their mouths coming together and parting, more desperately now, hungrier.

But suddenly, he stopped kissing her and his eyes sprang open. He gazed at her for several seconds before he said, "What are we doing?"

She peeked at him. Desire resonated through her. She wasn't really certain she had a voice. But having already misinterpreted their first kiss, she wasn't taking any chances with this one. "You tell me."

He sighed, lifted himself off the sofa and offered his hand to her, then pulled her up. "I don't know. And that's the point. I *don't* know. So it isn't right to go any further or do anything else until we know."

"Okay," she said, fighting disappointment but keenly aware that he was right. Their feelings for each other had changed. She wasn't willing to risk their delicate start by showing her distress or forcing him into something for which he wasn't ready.

"I don't want to hurt you, Liv," he said, backing

away from her as if not knowing what to do. "And if we jump into something, we both know one of us could get hurt. So, I just don't think this is right."

"I said it's okay."

He faced her. "Really?"

She smiled. "Sure. Get a grip, Josh. I'm not all that fragile."

Trying to be casual, she glanced around. It was too early to go to bed. But even if it were midnight, she didn't think either one of them would sleep just yet. Besides, she wanted him to be happy that he had kissed her, not stressed out and confused. They needed to do something normal, something simple that would bring them back to being friends again.

"You want to play cards?" she asked softly.

He heaved a heavy sigh. "Probably."

"Good," she said, pushing herself off the sofa to go and find the things they would need, not merely to save him the trouble, but also to give him a minute to collect himself. Unfortunately, because they were in a sparsely decorated living room, there wasn't any place to look for cards, or games, or anything that might entertain them.

"What do you want to play?"

"Pinochle?" he asked, apparently not sure if she knew the game. "In the family room?"

"Sounds good to me."

He led her into a back room that was decorated with an older brocade sofa and chair. A game table sat in front of sliding doors that opened onto a night-darkened patio. She found cards in a drawer of the cabinet that stood between two of the four matching bookcases lining the far wall.

"Want to play with a dummy hand?"

She shrugged as she made her way to the table. "I don't know any other way to play with only two people."

"Okay," he said, sounding more in control and happier now.

For the first half hour Olivia labored just to remember the game and Josh beat her soundly. Then she got a good hand, made fifty points and instantly shifted the direction of the score.

Before either of them knew what was happening, they had forgotten all about the kiss, forgotten they were struggling with an "almost relationship" they weren't sure should even happen, and forgotten they were trying to make lifetime decisions in what amounted to little more than forty-eight hours.

"I could stay tomorrow," she said, studying her cards, trying to decide if she should bid.

"So you said."

"Yeah," she agreed distantly, still preoccupied.

"Are you sure you want to?" Josh asked quietly.

The tone of his voice implied that he wasn't asking because he needed her help, or out of consideration for her interview plans. He was asking if what they were doing was more or less continuing their experimental relationship.

All she had to do was think about the feeling that roared through her whenever he kissed her and Olivia knew it wasn't yet time to give up. "Yeah, I'm sure."

He caught her gaze. His black eyes glistened with unfulfilled desire. "Good."

Holding the gaze of those brilliant onyx orbs, she fought the urge to swallow. If the look in his eyes was anything to go by, the man wanted to devour her. But, if this wasn't the time to give up, it most certainly wasn't the time to be a coward, either. She knew why she was staying. She knew their making love was inevitable. She knew she wanted it as much as he did, and she wasn't going to be unfair and pretend otherwise. "Good."

Those words confirmed their unspoken agreement and they continued playing cards. After only a few minutes, Josh said, "You know, since you're not going to work in the morning, you'll have the whole day to yourself."

"I can sleep in," she said, as if the concept were totally foreign to her.

"Yes, you can."

"I can't believe it."

Though he had been examining his cards, her tone confused him and he looked at her. "Why not?"

"I've worked every day of the last five years. The morning after I graduated community college I was at my first job. When I got my position at Hilton-Cooper-Martin Foods, I didn't take a break. Because I had to give a month's notice at the law firm, I couldn't even have a day off."

"You went right from one job into another?"

She shrugged and gave him a sheepish smile. "Seems to be the story of my life."

That troubled him more than being unexpectedly consumed with the need to make love to her on the sofa. Not because it sounded like she was hinting that she didn't give things proper attention. What she was really saying was that fate frequently didn't give her the luxury of time for thought. Now, as far as their changing feelings were concerned, he wasn't, either.

At eleven, Olivia went to her room. Josh stayed downstairs, locking doors, checking windows. Arousal blossomed low in his belly when he passed her bedroom door, but he ignored it. He wasn't sure what was happening between them, and because of that he didn't want to push the sexual aspect of their new relationship. The very last thing in the world he wanted to do was hurt Olivia. No matter what she said about not being fragile, he sensed she was very vulnerable and that if he made the wrong move or tried for too much too soon, he would hurt her. He had to make sure she genuinely understood and wanted the kind of relationship they were entering into or he wasn't entering at all.

Of course, given their age difference and that once she moved distance would preclude them from having anything permanent, she had to know they were contemplating a fling. A very delicious, very wonderful fling, but a fling all the same. And from her decision to stay tomorrow, he assumed she was saying she knew they would be taking this one day at a time. With no guarantee of even another twenty-four hours.

Which suited him perfectly.

In the morning, he rose alone. He ate breakfast alone. He drove to work alone. He had done that every day for the past five years, but today it felt odd, unnatural. He chalked that down to his growing familiarity with Olivia and even counted it as a positive thing. It proved he was getting accustomed to having her in his life, in his house—which was something he had never done before.

When he found himself watching the clock until lunch-time, and then becoming disappointed when he realized he had to eat alone, he started to think he was losing it. Or maybe going overboard. Or maybe growing to like her because he was tired of being alone.

That didn't sit well. Not at all. He thought he had gotten beyond the loneliness. But now he had to wonder if he had. A man couldn't contemplate entering a relationship with a beautiful woman like Olivia simply because he was lonely, yet he couldn't deny the sadness that slid through him thinking about Cassie.

Her sudden death had crippled him. He wouldn't deny it. He also wouldn't deny that he had jumped at the chance to come home when Hilton offered it. Though he didn't explain the truth behind his need to leave New York, he knew reacquainting himself with his family had resuscitated him, even though it had done little to assuage the emptiness.

The years that followed had rolled him into a nice, comfortable routine that made tolerable the dull ache of living without the woman he loved more than life itself. And lately the ache had shifted. Now he was actually able to remember Cassie and smile. He couldn't yet say the memories were pleasant. He couldn't yet say he was ready to sit down and think about that time in his life. But at least he wasn't consumed by shock and sadness every time he thought of how the twenty-five-year-old soul mate who had given his life meaning, had simply collapsed in front of him and never regained consciousness.

The pain he felt was why he had never entered into another serious relationship. Particularly not with someone who overwhelmed him with need. He might have survived the rejection of his first love and the death of his second, but he knew he wouldn't survive losing a third. All he had to do was look at his parents to realize love didn't last. But when he compared himself to his parents he also saw that he had somehow missed out on the gene that allowed them to move in and out of relationships the same way others changed socks. Once he acknowledged that, it was only a short step to concluding he couldn't get involved again. So he was careful, very, very careful.

Yet it was that very prudence that made a relationship with Olivia perfect. She was leaving. He wouldn't have time to become addicted to her. Knowing this relationship was temporary, he would always be preparing for the end, guarding his heart, shielding himself against that all-encompassing pain, so there would be no pain.

In the afternoon when Gina came into his office with an additional stack of résumés, he managed to get her to leave without discussing them and without explaining that Olivia would be picking her own replacement. Again, he respected the fact that Olivia didn't want anyone to know she was staying to help him. Though Gina knew Olivia had done that, he wasn't sure it was appropriate for Gina to know just how much help Olivia was giving him or how long she was staying—or even why she was staying. And right now, his biggest concern was protecting Olivia.

Which put her on his mind again. Solidly. At three o'clock, when he should have been intensely focused on feasibility studies written for Bee-Great Groceries and smuggled to Hilton-Cooper-Martin corporate headquarters by a source known only to Hilton Martin, Josh found himself intensely focused on his yellow number-two pencil. Although he'd been staring at it as if it held the secrets to the universe, he hadn't been seeing it. He was remembering kissing Olivia. He realized that he had gone from being her boss, to seeing her as a woman, to liking her, to getting jealous, to kissing her, to getting to know her, to kissing her passionately and desperately wanting to make love to her, to letting her sleep in, to missing the hell out of her.

The sequence was very logical. Unfortunately, it happened in such a short period of time that signals were going off in his brain, warning him that the situation might not be perfect, after all. It didn't seem right that he should be missing her this much. For Pete's sake, she was only a few miles away. At his home. Watching his TV. Sitting on his sofa. Her hair cascading over the hand she undoubtedly used to prop up her head. Her long legs stretched out along the brocade of his family room couch, clearly visible because she was probably wearing only a T-shirt and shorts.

The pencil snapped in two.

"Josh, I found one more candidate for you," Gina said, hurrying into his office, but when she saw the broken pencil in his hands she stared at him. "What the hell are you doing?"

"Nothing," he said, scrambling to bring himself back to the present. "These feasibility studies infuriate me, that's all."

"Well, they irritated my dad, too."

"You didn't read them?"

She shrugged. "With my dad, you, Ethan McKenzie and probably that nerd in the computer department poring over them, I think I can stick to what I'm good at. Taking care of the 'people' end of things. So, if you want to go over those résumés now, I'm ready."

"I haven't really looked at them," Josh confessed quietly.

"I know, I know, focused on the competition. That's fine. I'll catch you tomorrow."

"Great," Josh said, and went back to work when she left his office. But after only a few minutes, he found himself looking at the clock again. He told himself he wasn't obsessed, simply worried about Olivia getting into the office without anyone seeing her. At four-thirty, he ambled into the secretarial cubicle section of the third floor, ostensibly for a glass of water, but really to make sure everyone was leaving and no one was staying behind tonight—of all nights—to work overtime.

When he was sure the floor had cleared, he went back into his office and again tried to work. But at five-thirty he made a sweeping tour of the executive offices that rimmed the floor. With the exception of Ethan McKenzie, everybody had gone. Knowing Ethan was probably researching something and wouldn't be out any time soon, Josh relaxed. But before he could get back to his office, Ethan's door suddenly popped open and Ethan strode out.

"Good night, Josh," he said, heading for the elevator.

"Good night, Ethan," Josh said. Ethan and Josh had been hired about the same time. Both had been labeled by Hilton Martin as being one of the next generation. Like Josh, Ethan was a good choice to be part of the team in training for when Hilton Martin retired. He was as dedicated as Josh and the two men even looked alike. Both were in their thirties. Both had dark hair. Both had dark eyes.

Ethan disappeared behind the elevator door and Josh went back to his office. He only had an hour before Olivia was expected to arrive. Since he hadn't done any real work that day, he knew he had to use the hour wisely.

But he couldn't. He paced, worried that she might take the wrong route and end up snarled in traffic. Then he paced because he realized he hadn't heard from her all day. With ten long hours of free time on her hands, Olivia most certainly would have gone over the events of the night before, maybe even the whole weekend. She could have decided this situation they were in was all wrong. She could have repacked her bags, written a note and left him.

She could be halfway to Florida by now.

He combed his fingers through his short dark hair at the same time that he heard the elevator bell ring. Unable to curb his curiosity, he ran out of his office and rounded the row of cubicles that separated him from the elevator. When the doors opened and Olivia walked out, he grabbed her upper arms, yanked her up against him and kissed her soundly.

"What was that for?" she asked when he finally released her. But Josh took great comfort in the fact that her eyes were bright and her cheeks were flushed as if she had enjoyed the kiss every bit as much as he had.

"I missed you," he said, realizing it was true, but absolutely appalled that he had admitted that. Sheesh. They had only been apart a few hours. Not only did it make him a wimp that he already missed her, but he shouldn't be saying things like this, making a bigger deal out of this relationship than it was supposed to be. He had to keep his perspective.

"Well, I missed you, too," Olivia said, walking away, toward his office. For four years he'd hardly paid any attention to her. Now, suddenly, she was dealing with a man who couldn't seem to spend enough time with her. It wasn't that she didn't like it. She did. She liked it a lot. That was what made her suspicious of it. Something that burned this hot, this fast always fizzled out and she didn't want this romance, if they had one, to fizzle. She wanted it forever.

The realization stopped her, and Josh nearly ran into her back. He prevented himself from doing so by taking her biceps in his hands, and having him touch her so easily brought tears to Olivia's eyes. She would have pressed her hands to her mouth if she hadn't realized the gesture would alert him that she was having a crisis. She didn't want this to end. Not ever. Because she loved him.

She loved him.

And this time she knew she loved *him*, not a fantasy.

"Come on," he said, nudging her forward. "I have a stack of résumés on my desk."

"Okay," she said, forcing her voice to sound as normal as possible.

She led him into his office, but when they reached the door, he caught her hand and took the lead, guiding them to his chair. He sat and pulled her onto his lap.

All the blood drained from Olivia's face and her heart thundered in her chest.

"I shouldn't have missed you so much today," he said, then dropped a light kiss on her lips.

She ran her tongue along them, unable to believe all this was happening, and, again, not sure she could trust it. After all, that comment demonstrated that *he* obviously didn't. And she knew why. She might have had four years leading up to falling in love, but he hadn't. He'd had two days.

"This thing between us is happening so fast that we're doing things out of sync," he continued. "Things we probably wouldn't do if we had a little time to enjoy it. So I'm thinking that maybe your moving to Florida tomorrow might not be such a good idea.''

She drew a long breath. ''The timing does seem a bit off.''

''Yes, it does.'' He stretched forward, reached around her and grabbed his telephone receiver. ''Why don't you call that law firm and tell them you're not coming?''

''Because I need a job, Josh. I have nowhere to live and not much money to get a place. That's why I'll be camping out with my mother and stepfather for the first few months. I can't afford the start-up costs of a new apartment.''

''Live with me for a few weeks.''

A few weeks? She looked at him, studying his dark brown eyes before she said, ''You almost sound like you think what we feel for each other might burn out.''

He shrugged and kissed her again, as if laughing at her. ''We have to be realists, Liv.''

Disappointment shimmered through her. She had been right to be suspicious of his feelings because it almost appeared he didn't have any. If she were to guess, she would say she might be contemplating a relationship, but he was planning a tryst.

She pushed herself off his lap and walked away from the desk. ''I thought you had résumés for me to look at.'' She wasn't going to let the pain of his proposition get to her. Though he could be less blunt and a little more optimistic, she accepted what he was saying. From his vantage point, they didn't know each other well enough to make a commitment. Heck, she agreed with him. But she also knew she loved him. *Loved him.* If she asked him to stay and asked him to move in with her, she would at least give him the satisfaction of believing it was possible that their feelings might not fade. And equally possible that those same feelings would grow into real love. After all, hers were already love...

But his weren't. And that was the difference.

She drew a quick breath. "Let's look at those résumés."

"Let's not," he said, not sounding one iota like the man she thought she had known for the past four years. He rose from his chair and more or less stalked her to one of his new cabinets, where he trapped her. "I don't feel like working."

"Well, I do," she said, and escaped by dipping under his arm. "I stayed here today to help you."

"I thought you stayed because you like me?"

"I do like you," she said, irritated because that was the problem. She liked him too much. She liked him so much she might be giving him the benefit of the doubt when she shouldn't be. "But I stayed to help you."

"Come on, Olivia," he groaned. "If you only delay your trip as long as I need help, we won't get the chance to explore what we feel for each other."

"Why not?" she countered, spinning to face him. "Aren't I worth a short drive to another state every once in a while?"

"Why should either one of us have to drive, and why should we settle for seeing each other only once in a while, when we could see each other every day, if you would just stay?"

"And why should I give up my interview and the chance for a really good job? Why should I put my plans on hold to accommodate you?"

"Because it's logical," he said, sounding exasperated.

"Logical for you."

"And you," he insisted. "You're not gone yet."

"But I should be," she said, realizing it was true. If she hadn't stayed around they wouldn't be having this argument now. She would have left with a clear conscience and she would be free.

"No, you shouldn't. We would both regret it if we didn't enjoy what we have while we have it."

Olivia struggled for breath. He hadn't said "Let's explore the feelings and hope they grow." He said "enjoy what we have while we have it." Though she desperately tried not to put words in his mouth, taken literally, that comment implied he wanted something quick, something easy. Or something that came without hassle or effort. And that wasn't the way love worked.

"We both might regret it, Josh, but I don't see you putting yourself out on a limb for me. It's so simple for you to tell me to drop everything while you 'enjoy what we have.'"

The more she thought about it, the more irritated she got. Because it was true. He really wasn't investing anything. He wasn't risking anything. He couldn't even ask her to stay around for longer than a few weeks. He wasn't merely telling her he didn't want it to work, he *expected* this to fizzle.

He expected them to fail.

Tears sprang to her eyes and she felt like a colossal fool. "You know what, Josh? I can't do this tonight," she said, and turned and ran out of his office.

Her tennis shoes made a soft sound beating along the carpeted floor as she all but ran to the stairwell. She wasn't so foolish that she would take the elevator.

In the time she waited for it to arrive, Josh could catch her and probably talk her out of everything because she was such an idiot when it came to him.

"Olivia, wait!" he called, obviously only a few steps behind her, but far enough that he couldn't catch her arm.

She heard the desperation in his voice but chalked it up to his fear of losing something he wanted to try, not something he wanted to keep, and she forced herself to continue on, to walk faster. She reached the stairwell door and slammed her hands on the spring-action panel that opened it, then she started to run down the steps.

After she heard the door close behind her, she expected to hear the sound of it opening again and the sounds of Josh's loafers pounding down the stairs, but she didn't.

Apparently, she wasn't even worth the trouble of following.

Chapter Eight

Josh ran to the elevator, thinking it his only hope for catching Olivia. He punched the button, but nothing happened. It took a full minute for the stupid car to travel up from the first floor. By the time it arrived he wasn't merely angry at the delay, he was close to panicked.

He jumped inside and again punched the button until the door closed. When it reopened on the first floor, he ran to the glass entryway of the building and was just in time to see Olivia's little blue car driving out of the Hilton-Cooper-Martin Foods parking lot.

"Hey, Josh."

Josh squeezed his eyes shut, then faced his extended family with a halfhearted smile. "Hey, Gina. Uncle Hilton." If there was a God, his cousin and uncle hadn't been standing in Hilton's first-floor office doorway when Olivia ran down the stairs. They hadn't heard her slam her way out of the building, or seen her running to her car. They hadn't seen *him* rushing to try to catch her.

"Rather than work tonight," Hilton said, motioning for his daughter to exit his office before him as he pulled the door closed, "why don't you have dinner with Gina and me?"

"I can't, I—" Josh said.

"You what?" Gina asked, stopping in front of him. From the expression on her face, Josh could tell she wasn't merely paying attention, his behavior also made her curious.

"Nothing," he said, suddenly feeling like a complete idiot. He had only once been this out of control about a woman and losing her had nearly destroyed him. He would never again deliberately allow himself to be that vulnerable.

"You know, Josh," Hilton said, "I don't really like the way you work all the time. You're family. People are starting to say that I must be a slave driver if my relatives have to be here until all hours. So just have dinner with us."

"Unless you have something else to do?" Gina said, giving him a speculative look.

Josh held her gaze. He knew she was asking him if he had plans with Olivia. Which he did, but Olivia had canceled them. She ran out on him. Not the other way around.

He also wasn't worried about leaving Olivia alone at his house. She had been angry enough when she bolted from his office that if she returned to his home at all it would only be to pick up her suitcases—if she didn't already have them in her car—and she would soon be on her way to Florida.

He took a long breath because the thought of never

seeing her again gave him a tight band of pain around his chest. But the very fact that it gave him a tight band of pain proved he was right. They had gone too far, too fast, and it was wrong. Otherwise, he wouldn't be this out of control. He wouldn't have this feeling of helplessness. He would be sensible and logical and happy.

He wasn't happy.

"Yeah, I would love to have dinner with you," he said.

"Well, let's go, then. I'll buy," Hilton said, talking in a steady stream because he apparently didn't have a clue that Josh was entrenched in a personal crisis. "There's a new place on the other side of town. Great food. Do you want to ride with us or do you want to drive alone?"

"I'll drive myself," he said, and just those words strengthened him. He felt like a man getting some semblance of order back in his life. A man who didn't fall apart over a woman. "I'll be right behind you."

He followed his uncle to the new restaurant and met him and Gina in the lobby. Of course, Hilton Martin didn't need reservations and they were immediately seated. Once they had ordered and everything was settled, he caught Gina's gaze several times, assuring her that he had nowhere else he should be because as far as he was concerned, he didn't. By the time dinner was over and he had driven home, he didn't feel the slightest twinge of guilt or regret. Olivia had walked—run—out on him. He didn't have anything to feel guilty about.

Until he found the note from her on his kitchen table. Because they hadn't accomplished the work she had promised they would, she had decided to stay another day and had rescheduled her interview for the following week.

And she apologized.

Josh sat at the kitchen table and rested his head in his hands. Why did he feel so damned guilty? Why did he want to run upstairs and beg her forgiveness when he hadn't done anything wrong?

Why was he so out of control, when, really, he had only started getting personal with the woman two days ago?

Angry with himself, he didn't go to her room that night or see her the next morning. She didn't call to confirm her plan to meet him in his office at six o'clock that evening. She simply appeared at his office door.

"Hi."

Josh pushed his chair away from his desk and looked up at her. "Hi."

"Sorry about yesterday."

"I think it was my fault," he said carefully, not entirely sure what he had done, but also knowing *his* Olivia wouldn't run out on anybody without good reason.

"Or maybe both of ours," Olivia suggested, smiling slightly.

"Maybe."

"I, uh, used the computer in your den to type up a bunch of notes about the filing system and other things I do," she said, producing a disk from her jeans pocket. "I'll just take this out and print the pages, then we can go over them if you like."

"Okay."

"Okay," she said, and walked to her desk. Josh sank into his office chair and squeezed his eyes shut.

Blowing her breath out on a sigh, Olivia turned on

her computer, waited for it to boot up, then inserted the disk. All the while she counted the minutes until she could leave, because being here was difficult and embarrassing. She'd virtually asked the man to marry her because they had shared a few kisses. The only logical excuse she could give for that behavior was that she was scared. She didn't want to get hurt. She didn't want to cancel her plans and move in with him, only to have him realize six months from now that he didn't want her forever, the way she wanted him.

So though she spent the better part of the day making the itemized list of information that explained her job, she also used the first two hours to think this through and came to the conclusion that the smart thing to do was to leave. Soon. After they reviewed the résumés for her replacement, she would breeze through these notes as quickly as she could with Josh, then get into her car and head for Florida.

She pulled her document onto the screen, ran a final spell check, then set it to print. But rather than go into Josh's office while it printed, Olivia stood by her desk until it was finished, found a thin binder and inserted the pages.

Satisfied that Josh would learn more from her notes than he could from her trying to show him her job, Olivia took a deep, life-sustaining breath and walked toward his office door. But when she reached it, she stopped because he sat with his back to her, holding a picture, staring at it.

A quick glance at the bottom row of the bookcase behind his desk revealed that the picture of him and Hilton Martin was still propped beside the keepsakes he had pertaining to his time employed by his uncle. Which meant the picture he held had to be the one with

Hilton Martin and the man Olivia assumed was Josh's father.

"Is that your dad?" she asked.

He swiveled his chair around and faced her. "Yeah, actually, it is."

"I noticed a picture like that at your house, and then saw this copy here Sunday morning," she said, slowly stepping into the room. "You look just like him."

He smiled ruefully. "Yes, I do."

"He worked for Hilton-Cooper-Martin, too?"

"Yeah," Josh said, returning the picture to its original place. "Did you print those notes?"

"Yes," Olivia said. She casually handed him the binder, but her heart plummeted. If he would talk about his father, she could admit to him that she understood something about his workaholic tendencies. She could even tell him she recognized his fear that the way he drove himself might make it impossible for him to have a long-term relationship. After the way he'd kissed her, she knew he couldn't be worried about their age difference. His work habits were the only reason she could think of that would make him automatically assume their relationship would fail—maybe his other relationships had failed because he worked too much. But if that was the case, she believed a romance between them wasn't as doomed as he predicted. She understood how he worked, why he worked. She wouldn't fault him for it. So there could be no automatic assumption that they would fail.

Of course, he didn't know that. She hadn't yet found a way to slip it into the conversation. Discussing his father had almost opened the door, but he had changed the subject before it really got started. Still, there was no law that said she couldn't bring it back.

"Where is your dad now?"

Without looking at her, Josh said, "Nevada."

"Why did he quit?"

Josh peered up from the binder Olivia had handed him. "He didn't. He left without saying anything to anybody. Eventually Uncle Hilton took him off the payroll."

"You think he was fired?" Olivia speculated, taking the seat across from his desk. "Is that why you work all the time? Because you don't want to get fired like your dad did?"

Josh sighed and continued to flip through the pages of her newly printed notes, obviously doing a quick review. "Olivia, don't make a bigger deal out of this than it is. My dad left us for another woman—which didn't really sit well with my mother, who just so happens to be Hilton Martin's sister. Given that I'm Hilton's relative this time around, I'm not worried about how my relationships are going to impact my job."

Though she didn't show any physical signs, mentally Olivia deflated. She was so sure that the way he worked or his loyalty to Hilton-Cooper-Martin Foods was the reason he was afraid to commit. Or part of it. But if he wouldn't talk about it, then she wouldn't push him. Though she hated leaving this unresolved, she didn't want a man who didn't want her. She had already wasted four years of her life on this nonexistent relationship. It was time to move on.

"Whatever," she said, giving him a small smile so that they could close the discussion amicably and she could leave with at least a modicum of her dignity intact. "Do you like the binder?"

"So far so good," he said happily. "Not only do you have all your duties listed, but you have dates and deadlines and all kinds of great stuff.'' He stopped, caught her gaze. ''Thanks, Liv. I really appreciate this.''

''You're welcome,'' Olivia said, warming all over and softening toward him again because he genuinely was a wonderful person. She knew that for real now. She wasn't only guessing or assuming as she had been before. Not only had he done some sweet, funny things over the weekend, but he had made confessions, told her about his life, his family.

It suddenly struck her that she knew a lot more about him than she realized. Gina had confided that Josh hadn't had an easy life, but Josh had also revealed things to back that up. His father had deserted him. His mother had been married four times, divorced three, and was currently failing again. Was it any wonder Josh was a skeptic about love? Worse, was it really fair for her to leave angry with him when he had every right in the world to be cautious? Could she really say she loved him if she left without giving him a fair chance?

No. She didn't think so, because the truth was she didn't understand one half of what Josh had gone through. Sure, she hadn't had the benefit of his money, but she had spent her entire life being loved. She had been her mother's pride and joy. She had witnessed her mother's loyalty. She had seen her mother win at love. She believed in the miracle of happily ever after because she'd watched it play out.

And she owed it to Josh to give him at least another day.

''You know,'' she began slowly, watching as he continued to flip through the instruction binder. ''If you don't mind waiting until tomorrow to go over those résumés, I would like to take you out for a drink to apologize for leaving you in the lurch last night.''

He peered up. ''That's okay. I already told you I was more to blame than you.''

''Then you can buy me a drink.''

He glanced at her. ''Are we back to playing the *Dating Game?*''

''Yes.''

''Why?''

''Because I like you and you like me.'' She paused for breath and to gather her courage. ''And we need more time to get to know each other and trust each other before we really do anything about it because we really don't seem to be on the same page emotionally. I now understand you're only being overly cautious, but last night I interpreted the things you said as insulting.''

''Is that why you ran out?''

''Pretty much.''

''It insulted you that I'm pragmatic?''

''Yeah, and you would think that I would know better, wouldn't you? I've worked with you for four years. I know you don't take anything for granted and you rarely take the path of positive thinking.''

''So you're going to stay another night and then come in here again tomorrow so we can look at these résumés?''

''As long as we follow the same rules we've kept up until now.''

''No funny business?''

He didn't specifically say no more kissing, but since their metamorphosing relationship was the bottom-line issue between them, Olivia guessed that was what he meant. But that wasn't what she wanted at all.

"No *hysterical* business. We can handle funny, we just don't do well when we cross that line."

"Okay. But, Olivia, we have to be practical. Even if we go for a drink, you're leaving soon. You said you don't want to miss the opportunity at the law firm. So we're not embarking on anything long-term here."

"Florida's not that far away, Josh."

He shook his head. "Maybe not, but most long-distance relationships don't work out."

"You don't know that," Olivia began, but she stopped because Josh was playing with his pencil, nervously tapping it against his desk.

"The truth is, Olivia," he said, raising his eyes until he met Olivia's gaze. "I'm not as concerned about a long-distance relationship as I am about the fact that I'm almost thirteen years older than you. Thirteen years," he repeated, his voice weighted down with the significance of that number.

Thinking they had already gotten beyond this, Olivia frowned. "That bothers you?" she asked quietly.

He nodded.

"Well, don't let it. We're both adults, Josh. We long ago passed the place where age matters."

For that, he smiled. "You think?"

"Of course!" she said, glad he had finally opened up. Now his hesitation made perfect sense to her and also was something she could argue and help him to resolve in his mind because that's the only place where it mattered. In his mind. "It's not like you're thirty and I'm seventeen. We're grown-ups. We're at the same place in our lives."

"Yes, we are."

"Yes, we are!" Olivia repeated, if only to assure he completely absorbed it before she slid them back into going out for a drink, so he could continue to see her as a woman he dated not the twenty-one-year-old hired to help him four years ago. "Now, let's go get that drink."

"Okay." He rose from his desk and motioned for her to exit before him, then walked with her in the parking lot to her car where he stopped and looked around as if confused. "It seems kind of dumb for both of us to drive to a bar, then get back into our cars and drive home."

"So, why don't we just go home."

"You want to?"

"Sure," she said, deciding that was an even better thing to do than getting him to see her as his date. He could already see her in the role of his date. Heck, apparently he could see himself having an affair with her. He just couldn't see them together, forever. If she wanted this relationship to be permanent, she had to show him that even thirteen years younger than he was, she had the same interests and wanted the same kind of life.

She caught his forearm and smiled. "Let's go home."

When they arrived at his house they ordered pizza, which they ate in the family room while watching television. Comfortable and cozy, they let the empty box sit on the coffee table and settled on the old brocade sofa. Before the first commercial in the first sitcom, Josh had his arm around her shoulders.

Olivia cast him a covert glance. He was as relaxed as she had ever seen him, and she suspected the age difference was probably the farthest thing from his mind. Which meant the trick to getting him to forget about it completely would be to behave as if their being together was the most natural thing in the world. She shifted a fraction of an inch to nestle closer and before the end of the first sitcom, her hand was resting on his chest.

Before the middle of the second sitcom, Josh's fingers were kneading her shoulder. Before the beginning of the third sitcom, Josh's hand had slid to the spot just above her elbow and his fingers brushed against the side of her breast. And before the end of that same program, they were kissing passionately.

Without warning, they seemed to go from flirting, to kissing, to a passionate embrace that entwined their limbs and numbed their common sense. While his hands raced over her, his lips and tongue consumed her, and every inch of her skin vibrated with need. Feelings and sensations mixed and mingled until they were one distinct emotion-driven yearning. She ached for his possession.

"Stay in Georgia a few more weeks?" Josh begged against her mouth. "Jeez, Liv, you can't just leave and give this up."

He specifically said *a few more weeks* again, and though Olivia ached for him, and was also very understanding of his hesitancy due to the age difference, she couldn't stay under a deadline. Unless he gave her an open-ended possibility, at the very least the contemplation of a long-distance relationship, she couldn't agree.

"I can't stay without a good reason."

He slid his palm up the curve of her waist and rested it a fraction of an inch away from the underside of her breast. "I think we have a good reason."

Already near spontaneous combustion, Olivia fought a shiver as she inched away. Far enough that she could

see his face and said, "Can't you even give me one
tiny word of assurance that things *might* work out for
us?"

His frown deepened. "You want me to tell you today, right now, after three days of getting to know each
other, that we're going to be together forever?"

"I don't want you to tell me that you know for certain we'll be together *forever,* Josh."

With his fingers setting flickering flames everywhere
they touched and his lips still whispering against hers,
Olivia knew it was too darned tempting to say yes to
anything he wanted without proper thought. She
bounded from the sofa, paced for a couple of seconds,
then pivoted to face him. "I just want to know that
you're going to try."

"No. You might think that's what you want, but
really listen to what you're saying. Whether you realize
it or not, what you're asking for is a commitment,"
Josh said, sounding as if he were sorting through all
this and drawing conclusions that didn't make sense.
"In fact, it seems like you want me to ask you to marry
me." He shook his head. "After three days and two
make-out sessions, you want me to ask you to marry
me?"

Olivia gasped. "It's not like that!"

"Yes, it is," Josh insisted. "Because that's the only
way I can really give you assurance."

"Okay, Josh, there's no reason to raise your voice."

"I didn't raise my—" He stopped, realizing that, in
fact, he was shouting. He realized he felt trapped. Then
he realized there were huge tears clinging to the edges
of Olivia's eyelashes.

He felt the same panic as when she slipped out of
his reach and left the building the night before. "Oh,

God, Olivia, don't cry.'' He sprang from the sofa and put his hands on her shoulders, intending to pull her to him to comfort her. Instead, he pressed his lips to hers and suddenly he wanted to devour her. Everything about her called to him in an elemental way that didn't merely turn off his common sense and reason, it completely did away with them. Struggling for discipline, he refused to let it happen this time. With a monumental effort he restrained himself.

Then the strangest thing occurred. He began feeling a hundred different emotions he could neither define nor describe. He felt older, smarter, in control—with no thought of losing her—and he recognized that wasn't simply because he was holding on to sanity with both hands. This strange phenomenon was also transpiring because he was getting to know Olivia. He had an innate sense that he really could trust her, that they were equals, that he didn't have to worry that she would hurt him.

But when he pulled back and gazed into her eyes, he saw Olivia was feeling things, too, except hers were different. Worse, he could tell from the look in her eyes that this wasn't new, but familiar for her. And not only were the emotions familiar to her, they were deeper, stronger.

She loved him.

She *loved* him.

Chapter Nine

Josh didn't even have to say what he was thinking. Olivia could read the recognition in his expression and the way he backed away from her as if bewildered.

"Olivia?"

She licked her suddenly dry lips. "What?"

He combed his fingers through his hair. "Liv, you're not...we're not—" He stopped and drew a short breath. "Okay, I'm going to be straight with you. I only started this relationship because I thought you were interested in something completely different than what it seems you're interested in. And it's because we're talking about two different things that I'm stopping this before one of us gets hurt. I've never had a relationship that lasted. I can't give you any kind of assurance that this one will, either, because if we go by my past experience, we've got a few good weeks— if we're lucky, months—but that's it."

"Maybe that's because you've dated all the wrong people."

"Or maybe it's because I'm not good with relationships."

Studying his face, seeing he was very serious, and that his conclusion seemed to make him as sad as it made her, Olivia said, "You always sell yourself short."

"Not on this."

"How can you say that?" she asked, completely baffled. Clearly, he liked her and wanted a relationship, enough that he was willing to try to look beyond their age difference. But not enough to think of it as permanent. And the worst of it was now that he knew that she did want something permanent, he was acting as if she scared him to death.

"I've had my heart broken twice. Once was my fault. The other time was more like fate, but if I hadn't had my head in the clouds I could have prevented it."

"You can't judge everything by what happened in the past."

His eyes narrowed in confusion. "If you can't judge by past experience, what the hell do you judge by, then?"

She shrugged. "The past. But differently. You learn from your experiences, they aren't supposed to terrify you."

"I'm not terrified."

"I never said you were."

"But you implied it." He drew a quick breath. "Olivia, you're not going to talk me out of this like the John Travolta hair or the sans-a-belt slacks. This isn't something you can fix. And before we get into a fight that neither one of us can win, I think I better go to bed. We'll both get a good night's sleep and in the morning what I'm telling you will make a lot more sense.''

He strode out of the room without waiting for a reply and Olivia watched him leave. When he was gone she fell to the old brocade couch in abject misery. Every time she tried to make this relationship work, to give it a fighting chance, things somehow got worse. Knowing she wouldn't be able to sleep, she gathered the pizza box, paper plates and glasses they had used, and then tidied the kitchen. But when she was finished, she wished she hadn't because it caused her to see something important she had been missing. What she had inadvertently done was make herself look like she was moving into his house, trying to become his wife by playing the role.

It was no wonder he was frozen with fear. First, she virtually pushed herself at him at Hilton's party, now she had all but taken up residence in his home. He wasn't reading her behavior incorrectly. He was summing everything up very accurately. And she saw what he was saying. It really did appear like she wanted ''happily ever after'' after only a few days.

It was no wonder he bolted.

The next morning she awakened about the same time he did, but again let him eat breakfast alone and leave for work without seeing her. She wasn't trying to change the impression she had given him. She knew the battle was lost. If she had reviewed the résumés with him the night before she would have declared defeat and quietly driven to Florida. Because she still had résumés to review, she spent the day walking around the mall, not thinking about him or how awkward everything had become, but rather focusing on how good things would be when she got to Florida.

* * *

That night with Josh, Olivia ran through a quick, cool session of explaining the ten pages of notes about her job. Then she reviewed the résumés he had received from Gina. She was friendly and insightful when it came to choosing her replacement, but she wouldn't come around to his side of the desk and she didn't meet his eyes often. When she did, hers sort of blanked out, as if she had absolutely no emotion.

Josh didn't blame her. Whatever the hell they were going through, it was insane and confusing, and like him she had now chosen the path of neutrality to preserve her heart, which, it appeared, had already been bruised. He had a gut feeling that he should apologize, but he didn't know what he should be sorry for. He didn't want her to fall in love with him. He tried to be sensible, tried to make sure neither one of them got hurt. Yet, it looked as if she had gotten hurt, anyway.

"Well, I guess we're done here," Josh said, rising from his seat and stretching his back. "It's been a long day."

Olivia smiled, but Josh could see the smile didn't reach her eyes. "Yes, it has."

"Drink?"

She shook her head. "No. Not tonight. I'm a little tired."

"Oh," Josh said, sensing an opening and sitting again. "So you won't be heading out tonight, then?"

She shook her head. "No. We're getting done much later than I thought we would."

"I'm sorry, Olivia," he said, glad to have something concrete to apologize for to get this awful lump out of his throat. "I didn't realize it was almost ten o'clock. And we haven't eaten. Can I at least buy you dinner?"

"As long as we get something fast, and then go home, because I'm really tired."

He refused to acknowledge the tingle in his chest when she referred to his house as her home. He couldn't afford the emotions she offered him. He had been there. He had loved his father with his whole heart and soul and his father left. He had tried unconditional love in college and again with Cassie in New York. And both relationships had ended. He had watched his mother go through men as if they were Milk Duds. He knew the phenomenon of everlasting, unconditional love didn't exist, but since there were some marriages that worked, he wasn't fool enough to think there wasn't a less-intense option available. Surely, out there somewhere was a comfortable and workable love. A love that allowed people to marry, have kids and stay together.

Unfortunately, he wasn't experiencing it with Olivia.

He was once again finding that searing, passionate, out-of-control emotion that didn't last. Except with her it was the worst it had ever been. What he felt for Olivia, he felt twenty-four hours a day and if he let these feelings go any further, he would be swallowed up by them.

Then, when she left because passion this hot and emotion this intense always burned out, Josh wouldn't simply be alone again. He would be alone and he would be lonelier than ever because he would know what it was like to have her, but she would be gone.

So he wouldn't acknowledge the feelings that resonated through him. He wouldn't acknowledge the joy he felt knowing he had one more night of her company. Instead, he smiled. "Your wish is my command. Burgers and fries it is."

"Can we eat at home?"

That word again. That *feeling* again. He swallowed. "Yeah, sure. Why not?"

Because Josh had already given her a key to his house to use while he was at work, and because he would be stopping for their dinner, they went their separate ways. He used the drive-through at the first fast-food place he came to, then took a shortcut, hoping to surprise her and beat her home, but when he arrived Olivia was already there. And she had the kitchen table set.

"I thought we would eat in the family room."

She laughed. "You hate to eat in the family room."

"Not really," he said, then winced because he knew that was a lie.

"You hate clutter. You hate messes. You hate breaking your routine. You like to do things right. Eating at the table with a plate is right." She paused and smiled at him. "I'm not trying to take over your life. I'm not setting up housekeeping. I'm just tired of seeing you nervous and uncomfortable. So sit down and eat."

Josh cautiously sat. Nobody, it appeared, knew him like Olivia did, and, again, he wished with all his heart there was a way to make this work. But he knew there wasn't. And he couldn't risk the anguish when they failed. He knew that the only thing at the end of this rainbow was pain. He also knew he had just barely survived the last bout.

He distributed the burgers and fries, and got rid of the excess papers. Reaching for some positive small talk to assure she was comfortable, too, he asked, "So, you think the girl with five years' experience in the law firm is the one I should hire?"

"Hmm," Olivia said noncommittally.

Josh looked up from his burger. "But you were so enthusiastic about her when we were going through the résumés."

She shrugged.

"Did I miss something?"

"She's the best candidate, Josh, and she should be one of the people you interview. But, if you remember correctly, I also liked the guy who was working his way through community college."

Josh smiled. "Have you ever noticed you have a real soft spot for people who go to community college?" he asked, but as the words were coming out of his mouth, another thought struck him. Her first choice to replace her was the guy. She wanted him to work with a man. She didn't want him to hire another woman.

"It's not easy to have a job during the day and go to school at night," Olivia said simply. She was focused on her food; any other normal person would have thought she was only giving a portion of her attention to the conversation, but Josh didn't think so. There was definitely something on her mind. The possibility of him working with another woman had her simmering.

"No, I don't think it is easy to have a job during the day and then go to school at night."

"And spend your Saturdays doing homework or researching papers."

"I agree," Josh said, studying her, trying not to laugh because he had finally figured out she was jealous. *Jealous*. In his lifetime, he had been jealous. But he couldn't remember anybody ever being jealous over him. That was why it took him so long to recognize it. The feeling was new and oddly exhilarating. So exhilarating he started to enjoy it.

"But I also have to consider that somebody who is

going to school at nights and preoccupied with home-work might not be my best choice.''

Her eyes widened and her mouth fell open in dis-may. ''You're not even going to give him a chance?''

''I didn't say that,'' Josh said, rising from his seat. He took his plate to the sink. ''I merely pointed out that I'm going to have to consider that he might be preoccupied.''

With that he left the room, deliberately, to see if she would follow him. When she did, he almost burst out laughing. But he didn't. Stringing her along like this was too much fun, and his laughter would ruin the joke before he was done with it.

''If you consider anything, it should be the fact that this guy will be done with his associate's de-gree...probably well on his way to a bachelor's degree at the same time you're contemplating your next step up the corporate ladder. And he could slide right into your job when the time comes.''

''Oh, so now we're not hiring your replacement,'' Josh said, holding back a smile. ''We're hiring mine.''

She gasped. ''I didn't say that.''

''That's what it sounds like.''

She combed her fingers through her long yellow hair in frustration. ''I'm not. All I'm saying is...''

He grabbed her and pulled her down with him to the sofa. ''I don't know what's funnier, the fact that you hate to have somebody disagree with you, or the fact that you have such a soft heart.''

Her eyes narrowed in consternation. ''And you have a black heart,'' she said, but she didn't pull away from the circle he created with his arm. He had effectively teased her into forgetting to be angry with him, for-getting to ignore him, forgetting to treat him coolly. If he thought he could make this relationship last, Josh would have been proud of himself. But even though he couldn't make it last, that didn't mean he couldn't enjoy the simple pleasure of being in her company for as long as he had it.

"I don't have a black heart. I'm just trying to be a realist."

"No, you aren't," Olivia said in a huff, crossing her arms across her chest, though, again, she didn't move from the circle of his embrace. "You just want to hire an eighteen-year-old named Bambi."

"It does bring all kinds of possibilities to the mind, doesn't it?" he said, grinning.

She punched his stomach. "You're impossible," she said, then bounced from the sofa and stormed into the kitchen.

"Hey, don't go away mad," he said, and when she was out of earshot he burst out laughing. Then he bounced from the sofa and followed her.

"Really, Olivia, what difference does it make if I hire an inexperienced woman?"

"It doesn't," she said, and raised her nose in the air as if she didn't care. "If you want to be behind and have to keep track of everything yourself, that's fine with me."

"Good. Because what I was really thinking was I should hire Bambi to be like a personal assistant and get some older, more experienced woman to actually do the work. I could put her in a back room, or maybe a steno pool, so that no one figured out the truth. That way I could still give Bambi raises."

Olivia glared at him. "You pig."

"You gullible lamb!" he countered, and this time he did burst out laughing in front of her. "What do you think I am, an idiot? I saw how much work you do. I'm not going to hire somebody who can't help me. No matter how intriguing the name Bambi makes her sound," he said, managing to make his voice portray the interest he wanted her to believe he had.

She sighed with disgust. "You're a pig," she said, and stormed away again.

Josh followed right behind her, laughing. "I'm not a pig," he insisted. "I'm teasing you."

"Yeah, right," she said, all but running into the family room, where she grabbed her sandals. She turned, about to go upstairs, Josh assumed, because that was away from him, and he caught her mid-spin.

"I am teasing you," he said. His words started out with the lilt of laughter still in his voice, but having her so close and with his hands wrapped around her, everything in his world and perspective began to change. How he would love to have this teasing and laughter in his life every day. How he would love to have *her* in his life every day.

"You're not funny," she said, sounding like a wounded puppy.

"I'm sorry," he said, but he wasn't. He really wasn't. He couldn't remember the last time he laughed as much as he had laughed tonight, or this entire week, for that matter.

"And you're going to pick someone decent to replace me?"

"I'm going to pick someone decent," he assured her.

"You're not going to make me look like an idiot and replace me with a Bambi who may or may not even know how to type?"

"I think what you're really worried about is that an

eighteen-year-old Bambi might do better than you and make you look bad.''

Her eyes narrowed in warning.

"Okay. Okay, sorry. No more teasing."

He brushed a light kiss against her lips, intending only to end the moment properly, and this time he did exactly as he planned. The kiss didn't extend beyond what it was supposed to be. He kissed her and he pulled back. Regret and disappointment flooded through him, but so did the memory of trying to put his life together after Cassie.

She stepped back. "I guess I better go to bed."

"Yeah, I'll see you in the morning."

"I don't think so. I'm not sure I'll get up in time to say goodbye before you go to work, and I'll be on my way to Florida before you get home."

That hurt him, but he didn't let any of his distress show in his expression. "I could wake you up or wait until you got up before I left."

She smiled but shook her head. "That's okay."

Josh's heart sank. He wanted her to stay. He really wanted her to stay. But he couldn't promise her anything and she was too young to settle for nothing.

"Okay," he said, taking a pace back to give himself something to do so he wouldn't try to reach for her again. Desperation resonated through him, but he refused to give in to it. "Then this must be goodbye."

"Must be."

"Goodbye."

"Goodbye," she said, smiling slightly, as if remembering pleasant things from the past instead of the awkward few days they had just lived through. She drew a long breath and Josh was sure she wanted to say something else. But she didn't. She turned and walked out of the room.

"Olivia!" Fear overwhelmed him. Cold and clammy, it rippled down his limbs, through his chest, freezing his breath in his lungs.

She turned. "Yeah?"

"I...I..." *Like you...Love you...* Something. He wanted to say *something,* but he didn't know what. He couldn't promise her anything except maybe heartache when they separated. So it was pointless to make declarations that might only haunt her once she was on her own again.

He cleared his throat. "I wish you the best of luck in your new job."

Chapter Ten

"I want my job back."

"Olivia, are you sure?" Gina rose from her seat and rounded her desk to stand directly in front of Olivia. "It took you an entire year to make this decision. Do you really want to take it back?"

Olivia didn't hesitate. "Yes."

"Oh, Olivia, let's think this through."

Olivia shook her head. "There's nothing to think through. Your cousin was on the verge of admitting he loves me last night, but something held him back. If I leave now and can only visit once a month, he's going to talk himself out of it." She chuckled. "Actually, I would guess that if I left today and couldn't come back until next month, he will talk himself out of it before my first visit."

Gina drew a long breath. "I can't argue that."

"So you're going to give me my job back?"

Gina looked at Olivia intensely and Olivia steadfastly held her gaze. "You're sure about this?"

"Positive."

Gina smiled suddenly, stepping out of the role of human resources director and into the role of friend. "You really think he's on the verge of cracking?"

"I think he cracked last night," Olivia said with a laugh. Relaxed now that they were talking as friends, she combed her fingers through her hair. "I know that in his thoughts he was admitting how much he cared about me. Now all I have to do is get him to admit it to me and to realize everything will work out between us."

"If it's any consolation, I think you're right. And I'm on your side." She paused and grimaced. "Anything I can do to make your transition back into your old job easier? I mean, you did tell everybody you were leaving because of Josh, and now you're back. What excuse are we going to use?"

"That things didn't work out in Florida," Olivia said simply. "Because they didn't."

"Without saying anything substantive," Gina suggested, "we could make it look like you had your interview, but didn't get the job."

"Or got the job and didn't like it."

"Or had a really awful boss who made you realize that you were better off with Josh."

Olivia frowned. "I wouldn't go that far."

"No," Gina said with a laugh. "Neither would I. Let's stick with creating the vague notion that a mysterious something went wrong and you came back to the job you loved."

"Let's try to keep it simpler, and more vague, than that."

"Okay," Gina agreed with another short chuckle. "So you'll be back Monday."

"I'll be back Monday."

* * *

When Josh arrived home at six o'clock that night, he wasn't entirely sure what to expect. Olivia's promises to him were kept and completed, so there was no reason for her to stay. And she had said she was leaving. They had even said goodbye. But he also knew that she didn't have an interview scheduled in Florida until the following Wednesday. If she wanted to, she could stay with him until Tuesday night, and part of him was wishfully thinking that something had come up, or she'd changed her mind, or she just plain hadn't felt like driving that day.

He shrugged out of his suit jacket and hung it in the foyer closet. Turning toward the kitchen, he began to smell something delicious, something like roast beef, and his heart felt as if it had stopped, then speeded up again.

She was here.

"Hi, Josh," she said, when he ambled into the kitchen. His first instinct was to grab her and kiss her hello. Instead, he let his eyes drink in the sight of her. In her tight jeans and simple sunny-yellow top, with her hair swinging and swaying around her, she looked delicious. Perfect. Every atom in Josh reacted to her. Every fiber in his male being wanted to make love to her. Every inch of him ached with longing to have her with him forever.

But that was the problem. He wasn't going to keep her forever. He knew that. And he also couldn't handle being out of control. Being out of control was what caused all the heartache. If he could figure out a way to take this relationship out of the realm of being explosively passionate and into the area of comfortable love, he could see at least something of a future for them. As it was, all he saw was a crash-and-burn ending. If it killed him, he had to shift them out of this passion and into a normal state, and he had to do it quickly, because he didn't have a clue how much time he had before she left.

"Guess what?"

He glanced at her cautiously. "What?"

"I'm not leaving."

His heart stopped. "You're not leaving your job? You're not leaving Georgia? You're not leaving my house? What?"

"I'm not leaving my job. I'm not leaving Georgia. But I am leaving your house."

Now the blood seemed to freeze in his limbs. He cleared his throat nervously. "What are you talking about?"

"I spoke with Gina today. I told her I had decided not to leave. She said I could have my job back."

"But I thought you didn't want anyone to know..." He paused and ran his hand along the back of his neck. "I'm confused."

She smiled prettily. "That's exactly what I intend to happen. I'm going to confuse everyone. I'm not going to give much of a story, just tell everyone things didn't work out in Florida and let them make assumptions about how bad it could have been over there if I would rather come back and work for you."

"You're such a charmer."

"Aren't I?"

When she motioned for him to take a seat at the kitchen table, which she had set with his everyday dishes and decorated with a fat pot of daisies, he did so. And gladly, because his legs were like rubber. He wanted to ask her what was going on, what this meant, but couldn't because she was acting so normal.

Or maybe he could because she was acting so normal.

He picked up his fork and peered down at the plate of food she had given him. Roast beef, mashed potatoes, carrots, green beans. "This looks wonderful."

"Thanks, I'm an excellent cook."

He glanced at her. "I never would have guessed that."

"Because I'm pretty?" she asked, but she smiled at him before taking her first bite of food.

"Yes...no," he said, changing his mind. "No. For a second there I confused *pretty* with *competent.* You're so competent in the office, I guess I don't see you in the capacity of being competent at home."

"A lot of people are multitalented," she said, handing him a basket of Italian bread.

"Did you make this, too?"

"Nope, bought it at a store. That's kind of another talent. I know where to shop to get the really good things."

"I can see that."

They ate in silence for only a minute before she very casually said, "You know, Josh, it's okay for you to think of me in different ways that just your assistant."

He ripped a slice of bread in half. "I know."

"Okay, just so you're comfortable with that."

"I am," he said, and suddenly realized what she was doing. It irked him that she felt she had to spoonfeed their relationship to him, then admitted to himself that he shouldn't be mad at her for something that was true. He wasn't a wimp and he wasn't afraid per se. He was just a realist. It wasn't wrong to be wary of a painful inevitability.

"When are you moving out?"

"Probably Saturday. Gina invited me to stay with her."

"With her and *Hilton?*" Josh asked, alarmed.

"I've been very good friends with your cousin for the past two years," Olivia said with a laugh. "I've always admired your uncle. But I'm not staying there long. Next week Gina and I are going apartment hunting. So I'll only be there a few days. Two weeks tops."

"I thought you said you didn't have any money."

"Your uncle Hilton was so happy to get me back, he told Gina to give me a big raise."

He set his fork down. "So, you're going to sign a lease for a new apartment?"

"That's what most people do."

"You're not planning on moving in with me?"

She shook her head, but she was giving him a really funny look. "Why would I?"

Knowing she was probably right—her getting an apartment was a better way for them to turn down the heat so they at least had a chance of trying to make this last—he cleared his throat and said, "At some point I just assumed that you would…"

"Move in with you?" she asked angrily.

"Yes," he said, puzzled about why he was making her mad.

"You know, Josh," she said, slamming her fork down. "Sometimes you make me so furious I could scream. You needed my help and asked me to stay, so I stayed. You told me you were afraid of a relationship and couldn't seem to even consider it unless we took things very slowly, so I shifted my entire life to accommodate you, and still you're not happy. What do you want from me?''

She asked the question but didn't wait around for his answer. Instead she bounded from her seat and ran out of the room. Stunned, Josh sat perfectly still for a good twenty seconds before he allowed himself to jump off his chair and follow her. But not only had she gone to her room, she had also locked the door.

He knocked lightly. "Olivia? Liv?"

"Just go away, Josh."

"No. I think we need to talk about this. Can I come in?"

"No."

"Please?"

She sighed so heavily he heard her through the bedroom door. "All right."

He waited the minute it took for her to turn the lock and gave her a second or two to walk away. Then he stepped inside. "I'm going to tell you this whole, ugly, sordid story and give you the option to change your mind about coming to work on Monday."

"Okay," she said cautiously, watching him as if he would explode.

"The thing is," he said, ambling a little farther into the room. "I'm sort of a jinx when it comes to relationships. That's why mine are short. That's why I more or less pick the people myself, and don't fall into things that are too complicated."

She stared at him. "Are you questioning this relationship because you didn't pick me, or because there are complications?"

"Neither…well, both. You see, the real problem is that I'm kind of out of control around you."

"I don't get it."

"I like you a lot."

She looked at him as if she thought he was absolutely out of his mind, and on most levels Josh supposed he didn't blame her for thinking that. "And that's a drawback?"

"Yes. Because I like you so much that I know exactly how much I'm going to hurt when you leave."

"So you insult me and confuse me. Is this a test? Or do you want me to leave now, so you can start hurting sooner?"

"When you put it that way, Olivia, it sounds really stupid. But it's not. Haven't you ever been burned by a relationship?" he asked, taking a seat beside her on the bed.

She shrugged.

He caught her chin with his fingers and forced her to look at him. "Haven't you?"

"Yes."

"And it was bad?"

"I didn't eat for three weeks."

"When I lost my last real relationship, I thought I was going out of my mind."

She peeked at him. "Really?"

He sighed heavily. "I've never told this story to anyone before, but I think you need to hear it to understand how I feel."

"Okay."

"Okay." He stopped long enough to smile fondly, because the memories that came to mind were unexpectedly good ones. "My first real relationship in college was great. And I honest to God thought LuAnn and I would get married. But after our senior year she just went her separate way and that was that."

"And she hurt you?"

"Yes. But more than that she made me see I wasn't a very good judge of relationships if I couldn't tell that we weren't on the same page emotionally."

"Makes sense. But the truth is, Josh, that failure was good because it taught you something."

"Yeah," he said, knowing that was true. He learned a great deal from his relationship with LuAnn, and if he had been smart he would have remembered the lesson.

"What about the other girl?"

"She died."

Olivia blinked rapidly. "What?"

"She died."

"Oh."

"She got pneumonia, but thought it was the flu. She put off seeing a doctor because we were always so busy. Every day she seemed to get worse, but insisted she simply needed to push through it. Then one day, she collapsed and died."

"Oh, Josh, that's awful."

"We were working on the same project," Josh said, rising from the bed and pacing to the window, because now the memories weren't pleasant anymore. "Actually, she was my boss." He ran his hands down his face. "She was my boss," he repeated, staring out at the darkness. "And she was brilliant. If you think I have wonderful ideas, you should have seen hers."

"That good?"

"Perfect. *She* was perfect," he said, his voice barely above a whisper. "I knew she was pushing herself too hard. I knew she was sick...."

"You didn't kill her."

"I know."

"She was old enough and smart enough to see a

doctor,'' Olivia whispered, feeling very odd and very uncomfortable. ''And old enough and smart enough not to push herself so hard when she was sick.''

''I know that, too.''

''She was your boss. You might have felt awkward telling her what to do.''

He nodded. ''I was.''

''And working *yourself* to death isn't going to bring her back.''

''That's not why I work all the time. I'm not a complete nut case.''

Olivia sat frozen, not sure what to do. ''I don't know what to say, Josh,'' she said, swallowing. She felt awful and shrewish for pushing him. She felt foolish and addle-brained for not realizing something serious haunted him. But it had been so easy to be distracted by the age difference and his being a workaholic that she had missed the obvious. Something serious haunted him.

''There really isn't anything to say.'' He turned to her and smiled ruefully. ''Life's hard.''

''Yes, it is,'' Olivia said, but she didn't know that with the gut-level certainty that he did. She had had a great life. A mother who spoiled her, a stepfather who loved her. Her own father had died when she was five, but because she didn't know him well, she felt the loss in a different way than the way Josh would feel the loss of a life partner.

As she processed that, many other things fell into place. Like why he worked overtime but never asked her to work with him. And even why he hardly noticed her. He hadn't merely had a failed office romance. He had lost the woman he loved forever.

Silence surrounded them while he stared into the

darkness, mentally miles away from her. Olivia ached for him. She absolutely ached for the fact that his past had been riddled with so much sadness that he had buried all his emotions and didn't want to feel anything. But she also ached because there was nothing she could do about any of it.

"We never did finish dinner," she said, and slid off the bed.

"Not hungry," he said simply, coming out of his private thoughts.

"I am," Olivia said, then walked to the door. She hoped that if she went back to the kitchen and finished her dinner, he would follow suit, but she was also dealing with a brand-new set of feelings. By pushing him into a relationship, she had opened the wounds of the last one. Regrets and remorse strong enough to keep him from loving again were not the kinds of pains anyone wanted to remember or relive. And she had forced him to do just that.

She led him back to the kitchen, and though he sat at the table with her, made interesting conversation with her and even helped her clean up, he didn't eat. He smiled, but he wasn't happy. He beat her in cards, but he didn't really care.

Something inside him had died when his girlfriend died. And nobody was going to bring it back to life. Not even Olivia. Because he didn't want it back. He had hurt enough for one lifetime.

She went to bed before he did and thought he would follow right after her. But she awakened in the middle of the night, heard a noise coming from downstairs, and went down to investigate. She found him sitting in the family room, watching a videotape.

Standing in the doorway, she saw twenty minutes of

a beautiful brunette working, laughing and making presentations. In the same way a mother chronicles the life of her child, the tape had been made hit or miss. The scenes stopped and started arbitrarily.

Paying close attention to the casual comments Josh made when he was filming, and the comments made by the people taping him with the woman, Olivia surmised this was the woman Josh loved. But she also noticed something very odd. All of his friends were workmates. His lover was his co-worker. There were no picnic shots, no holiday scenes. There were no segments of anything outside a very posh Manhattan office suite.

And that was when Olivia realized why Josh worked so much. Behind his desk, laboring over advertising and public relations problems, he probably felt very close to this woman.

Studying him as he stared at the TV screen, she also realized something else. In five years, Josh hadn't stopped loving the beautiful brunette with the big brown eyes and the confident smile.

And that was the real reason why he would never love her.

Chapter Eleven

When Olivia walked to her desk on Monday morning, it was as if she had never been away. Technically, she hadn't. She had been in the office almost every night the week before, and if she hadn't left Josh's house the day after he told her about his former girlfriend, she might have come in with him, again, over the weekend.

"Olivia!" Doreen James gasped, when Olivia rounded the corner to her workstation.

"Hi, Doreen."

"What are you doing here?" Small and pretty, Doreen leaned against the rough fabric wall of the cubicle and peeked over at Olivia who was pulling knickknacks and decorations out of the box of personal items she had taken with her when she left two Fridays before.

"Things didn't work out in Florida," she said slowly, cautiously, trying not to sound ill at ease about her return, though she was. She was worried how her co-workers would perceive her taking her old job back when she had been so eager to leave, but more than that, she hadn't spoken to Josh since their discussion. And she knew that conversation was probably going to be the most difficult of her life.

After realizing Josh still loved the beautiful woman in the video, Olivia tiptoed back to her bedroom and cried herself to sleep. Not because it was obvious he would never love her, but because she was responsible for dragging him through his pain again. She couldn't even imagine what it would be like to lose a lover to death, and knowing she had forced Josh through that pain again was excruciating.

Thinking it best to give him some space to get his bearings, she left his home Friday while he was at work. She knew he would remember that she was staying with Gina and realized that eventually he would call her to make sure everything was okay. Then she could apologize and explain that she hadn't intended to hurt him. At least twice he had mentioned that he didn't want either one of them to get hurt, but Olivia was so sure he was being pessimistic that she hadn't understood he had good reason to guard his heart.

But he didn't call, and with every hour that passed she felt more guilt-ridden and sadder, until on Sunday night she realized what had been before her all along. She shouldn't be here. She shouldn't have stayed. She should have gone to Florida. In fact, if she had left the week before as she had planned none of this would have happened. Josh wouldn't be grief-stricken and she wouldn't have a broken heart.

When she told Hilton and Gina that she was going back to her original plan, Hilton offered her tuition to finish her education if she stayed. She knew he had done it as an enticement, because she'd never had money enough after community college to go on for her bachelor's degree. However, the extent to which Hilton had gone to keep her reminded her of something else she had forgotten. This really was a bad time for Hilton-Cooper-Martin Foods. They needed her. She had volunteered to stay. She couldn't take it back.

"It's too bad things didn't work out," Doreen said, moving away from the cubicle wall.

"Yes, it is," Olivia said. She forced a smile for Doreen. "I really wanted to live near my mother and stepfather. It would have been great."

"But you discovered that the grass isn't always greener professionally?" Doreen speculated.

"Something like that." Olivia shrugged. "There's no place to work like Hilton-Cooper-Martin."

"No, there isn't," Hilton Martin said, stepping out of Ethan McKenzie's office. "But we're also very glad to have you back," he added, walking toward her desk. "We need you on the campaign to save our market share against Bee-Great Groceries. I hope Gina made it worth your while for you to take your old job again."

Olivia could have kissed him. With Hilton sanctioning her return and almost making it appear that they had approached her, not the other way around, no one would question why she was back. She wouldn't endure a day of gossip, questions and speculation from her co-workers in addition to the heartbreaking confrontation she faced with Josh.

As if on cue, the elevator bell rang and Josh strolled out, reading mail as he walked toward his office. "Good morning, Hilton." He paused, caught her gaze. "Olivia."

The way he said her name today was different. He packed so much sentiment and so much emotion into the word that it sent a shiver down her spine, but also things between them had changed. He had kissed her. She had kissed him. They had nearly made love twice. She knew his deepest, darkest secret. The secret he hadn't shared with anyone. Not with Gina. Not even with his uncle Hilton.

Holding his gaze, she swallowed hard and then said, "Good morning, Josh."

"Well, I have to get back to the executive suite," Hilton said, turning from the cubicles and walking toward the elevator. "I got another batch of feasibility studies," he said, not specifically admitting they weren't Hilton-Cooper-Martin Foods feasibility studies, but studies "procured" from the competition, though Olivia knew they probably were. "Josh, you might want to come down later and check these out with me."

"I'll be there in about fifteen minutes," Josh said.

"Make it ten," Hilton called as he strode away.

Josh faced Olivia. "I think the smart thing for us to do would be to go through all the correspondence from last week."

Olivia gave him a confused look because they had done that. The day they cleared the clutter from his desk, they had gone through every piece of mail. Josh's correspondence was probably more caught up now than it had been before her week away.

Obviously seeing her hesitation, he nodded toward his office and Olivia realized that he didn't want to work, he was providing an excuse and an opportunity to go into his office to talk privately.

Everything inside her stilled. This was it. She didn't have a clue what he would say. She didn't have a clue what she would say. But it was time.

To keep up the appearance that they were leaving the secretarial cubicle to work, she grabbed the new notebook that she had left in the top drawer of her desk as a sort of welcome to her replacement, and followed him into his office.

He closed the door, turned to face her and said, "Are you really as okay with this as you seem to be?"

He didn't appear to be upset in the slightest, and Olivia experienced a few seconds of confusion until she remembered that he had been working for Hilton-Cooper-Martin Foods for five years, which meant that his girlfriend had been gone for five years. She quickly concluded that forcing him to discuss his former love and her death probably had brought back terrible memories on Thursday night, and might have even caused him to grieve again over the weekend. But now he looked fine. Which he should, Olivia decided, feeling foolish for being so worried.

She squelched a sigh of relief and said, "Of course. I'm the one who volunteered to come back to work here, remember?"

"I'm not talking about work. I'm talking about us. I know I told you I would understand if you changed your mind about everything once you heard about Cassie, and I do understand, but I need to know that you're okay."

"I'm fine," she said slowly, cautiously, wanting to say this in such a way that he understood, but also in a way that didn't dredge up painful memories again. "I recognize that you went through a trauma that will probably keep you from having another relationship for a long time. I'm not an idiot, Josh. I'm not going to push you into something you don't want."

"When you left without saying goodbye, I thought you were angry with me."

"I'm not angry with you." If she was angry with anybody it was with herself for being thickheaded. First she had caused him to remember the most painful time of his life. Then, although the man had ignored her for four years, at the first sign that he might be interested in her, she had changed all her plans for him. And he still didn't want her. He liked her. He appreciated her as a secretary, but he didn't want her as a lover, a wife or even a girlfriend. It broke her heart to realize he loved somebody else, but he did. He might not be paralyzed with grief, but he still had feelings for Cassie and wouldn't love another woman until he let go. If he hadn't been able to let go in five years, Olivia had to acknowledge that he might never be able to let go and she had to move on.

Olivia forced a smile. "Everything is fine."

The door behind Josh opened and Doreen peeked inside. "Josh, Hilton's back. He wants you downstairs *now*."

"Okay," Josh said, smiling at Doreen. But after Doreen left, when Josh turned to look at Olivia, his smile faded. For a good thirty seconds he studied her and she realized that if she hadn't been wrongly preoccupied with Josh's grief *this* was the problem she would have been dreading. Things between them had changed. They had changed drastically. He saw her differently. She knew facts about him and his life that no one else knew. They didn't have the same relationship they had when she quit two Fridays before. And she could see in his eyes that he was realizing that, processing it and not quite sure he knew how to behave. After an entire week of getting to know each other, sharing confidences, having fun and even being romantic, it didn't seem right to simply act like boss and secretary the way they had for the past four years, but he didn't appear to know what else to do.

He seemed so torn, she almost thought he would let go of the knob and come over and kiss her, or say something silly, or at least acknowledge that though he wasn't over his last love he had some kind of feelings for her. The air was so thick with tension that her nerve endings tingled and she held her breath in anticipation. After all, five years had gone by since he had loved Cassie. Maybe he wasn't as mired in grief as either of them thought…maybe he was ready to let go.

But he didn't do anything. He didn't say anything that might have made her feel he was ready to move on. He didn't say anything that might have made her feel she hadn't been completely wrong to fall in love with him. Instead, he drew a long breath, gave her an awkward smile and said, "I'm very glad to have you back."

She nodded. "I'm glad to be back."

With that he walked out of his office and Olivia began sorting through the mail that had been delivered on Saturday. When she heard the elevator bell that signaled that he was on his way, she stopped sorting and stared straight ahead. The way he looked at her sent shivers through her. The way he smiled weakened her knees. His concern for her, when he was the one more hurt Thursday night, proved again that he was somebody worth loving.

No matter how hard she tried, she couldn't stop loving him. And now she was trapped working with him, at least until after the Bee-Great Groceries crisis.

* * *

Josh didn't return until after lunch. Olivia spent her morning productively, reversing their filing system to the way it had been the day she left. But she spent her hour-long break stressfully bouncing back and forth between dodging questions about the nonexistent trip to Florida and questions about how she felt about returning to work with Josh. Her nerve endings were frayed, her patience was gone and another problem had reared its ugly head. Unless she was one hell of an actress, her co-workers would soon realize she still loved Josh.

"So, did you get through this morning's mail?" Josh asked, passing her desk.

She nodded and rose to follow him into his office, pen and paper in hand. "Most of the things I could handle myself."

When she was inside the room, Josh closed the door. In addition to her already frayed nerves, Olivia got a sinking feeling in the pit of her stomach, wondering if this was the rest of her life. She didn't want be alone with him in his semidark office. She didn't want to have personal conversations that required closed doors. Because those things made her wonder about his motives and made her wish that maybe…just maybe…he had changed his mind, and she couldn't do that. She had spent four years pining for him, and thinking that she would spend another year or two or the rest of her life longing for his love overwhelmed her with sadness. She knew he would never love her.

But giving him the benefit of the doubt, Olivia remembered that he was having trouble figuring out how they were supposed to relate to each other, which could account for his atypical behavior. Since it was an unusual situation, she realized she couldn't fault him for it. So, she decided to ease them back into her normal routine.

"These are the letters that need your attention," she said, taking her seat in front of his desk. When he took the cue and sat too, she pointed out a specific piece of correspondence he needed to address.

As expected, he read the letter and quickly dictated a reply. Olivia immediately gave him another document, and, after reading it, he dashed off a response for that, as well. She kept up the steady stream of work until they got through everything in the mail stack, then, as she had in their former working relationship, she left his office.

She also left her cubicle at four-thirty when the other secretaries and administrative assistants quit for the day. Even though Gina stayed until five-thirty or six, and Olivia and Gina had driven in together that morning, Olivia wasn't waiting at her desk. Before she quit, she had gone at four-thirty with everyone else and she would do that again tonight. She meandered to Gina's office, sat in the reception area where job applicants usually waited for interviews, and read two magazines.

At six, Hilton came in to roust Gina from her work. "Is she still at it?" he asked Olivia, who set her magazine on a low table by her plastic chair.

"Looks like it."

"Well, let's get her the heck out of there, I'm hungry."

"I'm hungry, too," Olivia admitted with a heavy sigh.

"Great!" Hilton said. "Come on, Gina, we've got a live one. Olivia is starving. I think we should take her to the all-you-can-eat seafood buffet at the club."

Olivia's stomach nearly danced for joy. "I can handle that."

"And my dad loves having somebody to eat with," Gina said, laughing as she pulled her office door closed.

"It's no fun having money if you don't have anybody to share it with."

"You have lots of people to share it with," Olivia said, teasing him.

"I want grandchildren."

"He wants grandchildren," Gina said, rolling her eyes. "He wants me to take over the company. He wants me to do more out-of-the-office PR. I keep telling him he can't have everything. But he doesn't seem to listen."

Olivia laughed as she, Hilton and Gina walked through the first-floor lobby to the glass-door entryway. Crossing the parking lot, Gina kept up the conversation, teasing her father about the pressure he put on his only child, and though Olivia tried not to, she covertly peeked up to the third-floor window she knew to be Josh's. Of course, she couldn't see anything, but even if she could, she doubted he would be standing there hoping to catch a glimpse of her as she left. He didn't love her. He didn't want her. He wanted the old love of his life back. And she had to accept that.

Watching Olivia and Gina as they climbed into Gina's Mercedes convertible, Josh's eyes narrowed. He had wanted to have a more thorough discussion with Olivia about what had happened when he told her about Cassie, but he never got the chance, and it almost seemed she was going out of her way to make sure he didn't get the chance. Almost as if she had optimistically changed her mind again about their relationship—as she had so many times the week before—and she was avoiding him so he wouldn't realize it.

He was positive it was for the best when he discovered her gone when he got home from work Friday afternoon. He didn't mind that she didn't call that night or come over to finish their discussion. He certainly didn't expect her to drop everything to talk with him over the weekend. However, he had expected to talk this out today.

This morning when Hilton pulled him away to read feasibility studies, he went peacefully, believing they could finish their discussion this afternoon. But Olivia hadn't seemed predisposed to talk this afternoon. In fact, he had more than suspected she had used work as an excuse to draw them away from their personal conversation. Now she was leaving with Hilton and Gina. Probably going somewhere to eat.

He sat at the desk and rubbed his hands down his face. He wasn't really sure what he was going to say to Olivia, but he did want her to keep his confidences. And he hoped he hadn't hurt her. She appeared strong, happy, satisfied with her decision to stay, and though she claimed to understand that he didn't want another relationship, he wasn't sure she really meant it. He wasn't certain she hadn't stayed seeking a romance that wasn't going to happen.

When she arrived at the office the next morning, Josh was waiting for her, but, as had happened the day before, they didn't really get an opportunity to talk. With so many people working around them, there never really was a way to be alone except in his office. Josh also realized that no matter how private he made his office, he couldn't control Olivia's reaction. He decided this might be a conversation better saved for the end of the day when everybody was gone and the floor was empty of potential eavesdroppers.

At twenty-five minutes after four, he called her in and asked her to sit down. She immediately pointed out a work document to him.

Seeing the last of her co-workers wandering to the elevator, he caught her hand. "Olivia, we need to talk."

She straightened her shoulders and pasted a smile on her face. "I don't think so. I think you said everything that needed to be said on my last night at your house, then yesterday morning I confirmed that I understood."

He swallowed. She was so beautiful. He realized he could spend hours just looking at her. He couldn't even imagine how wonderful it would be to be married to her—to have her beauty, her sense of humor and her laughter around him twenty-four hours a day. But he was damaged goods. Not somebody capable of having a normal, honest relationship, and he didn't want her to get involved with him. Because she was so young she would ultimately find another love, a better love, and the best thing he could do for her was let her go. Even as that statement reinforced his conviction, it drove a spike of jealousy through him. But he ignored it. It was for her benefit that he ended this in such a way that neither of them would look back.

"I think we need to talk about why you stayed in Georgia."

"I stayed because I wanted to, Josh."

"And why did you want to?"

She gave him a puzzled frown. "What do you mean, why did I want to?"

"Did you stay because you wanted your old job back?"

"Yes," she said, frowning again. "You know I love my job."

"And that was reason enough to change your plans?"

"That and the raise...and the offer of tuition that I got from Hilton Martin," she replied, sounding angry. A few seconds passed as she apparently processed the real purpose for his questions, then her facial features hardened. "Why don't you just come right out and say what you're hinting at?"

"I hope you didn't stay for me."

Her eyes widened as if he had pushed her over the edge of temper, but she quickly controlled herself. "Josh, if you're worried that I'm going to attack you at the watercooler, relax. I'm fine. Everything is fine between us."

"I don't want you waiting for something that isn't going to happen."

Again, he saw a flash of temper that was quickly covered by calm. "I'm not going to be sitting around knitting sweaters."

"I mean it."

"So do I," she said coolly. "I told you. Hilton offered me tuition. I'm going to get my degree."

"That's good."

"You're right. It is good. It's a very good reason to stay and a very good beginning to a new life for me. You don't have to worry about me. I'm going to be fine. I'm not sitting around waiting for you."

"I don't want you waiting for me at all."

"Excuse me?" This time her temper wasn't as controlled as it had been and Josh knew he was skating on thin ice with her, but he needed her assurance that she really was letting this go. Not merely because he wanted her to move on and make a good life for herself, but also because he had spent five long years getting accustomed to being alone. He couldn't lose that fragile peace now.

"Olivia, I don't want you waiting for me at all." He stopped talking, rose from his seat and paced to his window, so he didn't have to look at her beautiful face. "I don't want to be in love. I don't want to get married. I don't want all those things that I'm just about certain that you want."

"You don't want them, or you're afraid of hoping for them because you're afraid of being hurt again?"

"I know you think you have this all figured out…and you might," he admitted, turning to face her. "But the point is, I like you enough that I won't let you hang around waiting for me."

"I would tell you to let me be the judge of what I will and will not do, except I'm not waiting for you."

"I hope you mean that." He said the words quietly, but they had an unexpected effect. She reacted with a quick jerk, as if he had slapped her.

"Josh, you're not quite the prize you think you are," she said, rising from her chair. "Thank you for behaving like a sanctimonious, conceited nitwit, because you just made my life a hell of a lot simpler."

With that she strode out of his office and Josh took three long breaths. He hadn't hurt her. He had made her angry, which was good. Now she wouldn't question the decision to separate their personal lives. Now she would move on. She would take Hilton's tuition money and get her degree and probably find a man who genuinely deserved her.

He sighed and bent his head to begin working again, satisfied that he had cleared things up between them for good. He refused to acknowledge the dull ache around his heart. It had been there for five years. He had felt it when he lost Cassie. He had had it when his father left. He knew this pain. He could deal with it. It would never really go away, but at least he could handle it.

Chapter Twelve

Furious with Josh, Olivia didn't walk to her car, she marched. Her feet pounded on the pavement. Her arms swung. The breath pushed in and out of her lungs. When she reached her vehicle, she jumped inside, turned the key in the ignition and screeched out of the parking lot. She was so angry and so preoccupied that she almost turned in the direction of Hilton and Gina Martin's home, but remembered that she hadn't ridden to work with Gina because she was to meet a former Hilton-Cooper-Martin Foods employee, Savannah Grogin, for dinner at a nearby restaurant.

Olivia didn't want to go. Not at all. But Savannah was an old friend who had moved from Atlanta when both of her parents died. Not knowing what to do with the bed-and-breakfast they bequeathed her, Savannah had gone to Maryland to sell it, but never returned. Part of Olivia was curious about the enticement. Another part wanted assurance that her friend was okay. In fact, she wanted the reassurance enough that she calmed down, forgot all about her conversation with Josh and maneuvered her car in the direction of the restaurant.

Because she hadn't left at four-thirty as she was supposed to, Olivia arrived to find Savannah already seated. The waitress walked Olivia to the table where a red-haired woman sat, but the woman did not look at all like Olivia's former co-worker. The Savannah she remembered was slightly chubby and had short hair. This woman was thin, almost tiny, and her hair flowed past her shoulders.

Preoccupied with the menu, the woman didn't look up so Olivia said, "Savannah?"

Savannah's eyes widened comically and she nearly leaped out of her seat. "Oh, my gosh! Olivia!" Though short and fragile-looking, Savannah grabbed Olivia in a strong, emotion-filled hug. "It's so good to see you."

"It's good to see you, too," Olivia said as both women sat on the bench seats of the booth. "You look wonderful!"

"Different," Savannah admitted with a laugh. "Owning my own business keeps me hopping."

"Well, I love your hair."

"Believe it or not, it's easier to care for it long like this," Savannah said while the waitress handed a menu to Olivia. "I'm so glad you could come."

"Oh, you know me, I never was much for working," she said, then felt weird having said it. Because it was true. She liked her job and she liked working, but she wasn't upwardly mobile. That's probably why Josh had questioned her decision to stay based on tuition from Hilton Martin. Getting her degree was a good idea, earning more money sounded great, but everybody knew she wasn't the type to compete for jobs, or to work twelve hours a day seven days a week. Having a life had always meant something different to her. That was why Josh had questioned her. He hadn't intended to make her mad. He simply knew a degree would not motivate her. True, he could have been nicer, but that was Josh. She'd lived with his male insensitivity for four years.

Relieved that he wasn't the complete idiot she thought, she smiled at Savannah. "I'm so happy to see you. I think a nice, relaxed evening with a friend is exactly what I need right now."

Savannah's brow furrowed. "Why would you need to relax? Did something bad happen?"

"It's a long story," Olivia said. She patted Savannah's hand. "And it can wait. I'm more interested in you. What in the heck made you decide to stay in Maryland?"

Savannah grinned. "I really don't know. I think I did it just because I was shell-shocked and confused, but now I'm glad I did. The business is doing well, and it helped me to feel connected to my parents. I also think that connection helped me to accept their deaths."

Olivia patted her hand again. "That sounds good."

"Yes. It was." She sighed. "Except now that I'm settled, I really am *settled*, and I have been getting these odd urges to have a baby."

"A baby! Oh, Savannah, that's great! I didn't even know you were dating somebody."

"I'm not," she said, then she grimaced again. "Olivia, the reason I asked you to have dinner with me is that I...well...I did something unusual."

"How unusual?"

Savannah nervously played with her silverware.

"Well, my brother works at a sperm bank, and I don't have anybody special in my life—"

"Oh, my gosh! You're thinking of getting pregnant using in vitro fertilization?"

"I had already made arrangements and—"

"Oh, my gosh! That's great!"

"You don't think I'm stupid?"

"Heck, no!" Olivia said emphatically. "They screen the donors. They're very careful…and you said you *wanted* a baby."

"I do," Savannah said.

"Then I think you should do it."

"Really?" Savannah asked carefully, but the color was back in her cheeks and the sparkle was in her eyes again.

"Absolutely," Olivia assured her. "You're doing something about what *you* want. You're not doing what everybody else thinks you should be doing," Olivia said, and her own words echoed in her head, convicting her. Going to college was a very good idea. But it wasn't *her* idea. It was Hilton Martin's. "And you're not just sitting passively waiting for life to happen to you."

"No, I'm not," Savannah agreed. "Just like you're not." She smiled at Olivia. "Gina mentioned on the phone this afternoon that you were going to leave Hilton-Cooper-Martin, but her father offered tuition money for you to get your degree and you're staying."

"That's right," Olivia said, feeling better about the tuition, because at least no one seemed to think she had stayed for Josh. That tuition was helping her to save face.

"So it looks like we've both found the directions for

our futures," Savannah said, toasting with her glass of water. "I would say that's reason to celebrate."

"Absolutely," Olivia agreed, but she could tell just from looking at Savannah that she didn't feel the same level of joy as her friend. Savannah had a deep-down glow, and unless just deciding to get pregnant made a woman look better than any woman in the rest of the world, Olivia could only assume that Savannah truly had made the right choice.

Olivia wasn't sure she could say the same.

She finished the dinner listening to Savannah and being excited for her because, frankly, Olivia had never seen anyone so ecstatic. Savannah had suffered the tragic loss of her parents. She'd moved from bustling Atlanta to tiny Thurmont, Maryland. She was a small-business owner now. She was about to become a mother. She had settled down. And it suited her. Actually, it suited her the way Olivia had always believed marriage and motherhood would affect herself. Savannah's cheeks glowed and her eyes sparkled. A degree didn't make anybody's cheeks glow, and though it might make some people's eyes sparkle, a degree didn't hold a candle to babies, a home and a husband who loved her and made her laugh and loved her cooking.

When Josh arrived at work the next morning, Olivia felt another wash of regret. In his black suit, white shirt and blue tie, he looked wonderful. Perfect. And it hurt her to know that they would never have a relationship....

No, it hurt her to have to look at him every day and know he didn't want her. Know he didn't want to sleep with her every night and wake up with her every morning. Know he didn't want her children.

She wasn't a silly woman. She wasn't a selfish woman. She might be prone to a fantasy or two, but she wasn't irrational. She wasn't so far gone that she couldn't make a judgment about what was plainly before her. She loved Josh Anderson and he did not love her. Being with him eight hours a day, five days a week was going to be torture.

She could not do it.

"You know that this is the rest of your life, don't you?"

Josh looked up from his work to see Hilton Martin standing in his doorway. As his eyes adjusted to the brightness of the light from the secretarial pod, he also realized that it must be very late because his office was dark. The only light in the room was the brass lamp to his right, and that only lit the square of space in which he read and wrote.

"If you're hinting that I work too hard, forget it!" Josh said, but he laughed as he stretched the kinks out of his back. "You're the person who gives me the assignments."

"Is that why you're here all the time?" Hilton asked, ambling into the room.

Hearing something odd in his tone, Josh studied his uncle's expression for a few seconds before he cautiously said, "Yes."

"I don't think so," Hilton said, taking the seat in front of Josh's desk. Olivia's seat. "I think you work because you're avoiding life."

Josh laughed. "Look who's talking."

"Exactly," Hilton said, catching Josh's gaze. "Look—really look—at who's talking."

"Okay, Uncle Hilton, I can see you're trying to

make a point, but I'm not getting it. And it's too late at night to beat around the bush. Why don't you just come right out and tell me?''

"Okay, Olivia not only quit today, she's on her way to Florida."

"Oh." That hit Josh like a ton of bricks, but he schooled his features so Hilton wouldn't see.

"At four-thirty she came into my office and talked with both Gina and me. She told us she needed to leave. Then Gina went back to our house with her so she could repack her car. When Gina returned a few minutes ago, she told me Olivia was on the road. She wasn't even waiting for morning."

"She's gone?" Josh said, because the darned notion wouldn't sink in. He knew getting her degree wasn't what she really wanted, but he also saw it as a good thing to do. He couldn't believe she would give that up... He thought she would stay. At least so he could see her, watch her accomplish her dreams.

"Yeah, she's gone, and, frankly, part of me wants to slap you silly."

"Me?" Josh gasped. "Why me? If anybody's leaving you in the lurch, it's Olivia."

Hilton waved a dismissing hand. "No, she's not. We've been preparing to replace her for weeks. You're the only person who hasn't kept up with the program."

"I will," Josh assured his uncle, forgetting the dull ache in his heart and the band of pain around his chest so he could get through this discussion like a rational, intelligent man.

"No, you won't. Because you won't be with this program unless you get in your car and try to catch her!"

Not sure what his uncle was driving at, or why he

would torture his only nephew, Josh didn't even react. Not a facial muscle moved. He wouldn't let any emotion flicker in his eyes. "Uncle Hilton, she's gone. You already told me you guys have been preparing to replace her. Why would I want to race down I-75 to catch her?"

"Because you love her, and because if you don't do something soon she's not going to want you."

"I don't love her," Josh insisted, if only because that's what he kept telling himself.

"Of course you do. I know you think you still love Cassie, but five years have passed, and though you might have residual feelings for her, you've adjusted. Little by little over the past years, you've let Olivia into your life. And I kept her around, looking for little excuses, but good ones, to prevent her from moving with her mother. I even pulled out the big gun of thousands of dollars in the form of a degree, because I wanted her here when you were over your grief so you would get the chance to see the obvious. But you just couldn't take that last step."

"No, I couldn't," Josh said, honest since Hilton apparently knew the truth. "I didn't realize you knew about Cassie."

Hilton smiled. "I know everything," he said, but relented when Josh gave him a firm look. "All right, when your mother told me that you were suddenly unhappy in New York when for years you had thought it was the most wonderful place in the world, I made a few calls to find out why. I didn't tell anyone what I discovered. I just made arrangements to bring you home."

Josh toyed with his pencil. "Since you apparently know everything, you should understand what I feel right now. You know about losing someone you love," he said, referring to his aunt Rayanne, Hilton's late wife. "And I haven't seen you move on. So I know you know why I'm not."

"Everybody's life is either a good example or a horrible warning," Hilton said, shaking his head. "From where I sit, you should be using me as one of those warnings, and you should know better than to waste your life like I did mine."

"You didn't waste your life."

"You don't think so? I have to bribe people to have dinner with me. I belong to a garden club so I can fill my house with friends when I want to have a party. I'm stifling my own daughter by simply giving her everything she wants and needs, so she doesn't want or need anybody else in her life. I'm an albatross, Josh." He paused and caught Josh's gaze. "And give yourself another few years and you will be, too."

"You think I should go after Olivia so I'm not bored," Josh said incredulously. "Or a burden to others?"

"Nope," Hilton said, then rose from his seat. "I think you should go after Olivia because she put a sparkle in your eyes that I hadn't seen for a long time. I think you should go after her because she adores you, and I think you should go after her because if you don't you will regret it. She's going to marry somebody one day, Josh. She's going to have beautiful children and make some man very happy. If it isn't you, it's going to be somebody. Can you handle that?"

He walked to the office door but paused and faced Josh again. "I know how hard it is to lose somebody you love. I know how hard it is to trust again. And I'm not talking about trusting Olivia. I'm talking about trusting life. After somebody you love dies, it's nearly impossible to trust life again. To trust that life isn't going to give you the best love in the world only to take it away from you.

"But if you don't take that step, some day you are going to wake up very, very alone. And you're also going to realize that your chances are gone. You won't have kids. You won't have a white picket fence. You may not even get a dog…but, worse, you won't have known long-lasting, forever love, because you won't have enough years left to try.

"This opportunity won't come around again. Not with someone like Olivia, who's not only smart and patient, she's absolutely beautiful. Two minutes after she sets foot on a Florida beach, some man's going to snap her up and he's going to be the guy who gets the blond, green-eyed princess for a daughter. Two minutes, Josh. That's all you're going to get. Then you lose.''

Chapter Thirteen

After his conversation with Hilton Martin, Josh couldn't work anymore. He told himself he was simply tired and drove home. But when he entered his foyer, he could smell the faint scent of Olivia's cologne that lingered in his house, and he knew he wasn't merely tired. He was dying inside. He loved Olivia. The truth was, he probably loved her more than he had loved Cassie, but that only made the fear of losing her all the more intense. It had taken him five years to get over losing Cassie. If Olivia died, he didn't think he would survive.

He stripped off his suit coat and hung it in the closet, then searched his kitchen cupboards for something to eat but didn't find anything. When he looked in his refrigerator, he realized he didn't even have eggs. He had nothing in his cupboards, nothing in his refrigerator, and he probably didn't have anything in his freezer, either. If he didn't work up the energy and ambition to shop soon, he would starve.

Then he saw the leftover roast beef and his hand hesitated above the container. But he told himself to quit being stupid. It was roast beef. It wasn't a sign from God, a sign of love or even a sign of affection. It was food.

He took it out, microwaved it with some leftover potatoes and sat down at the table with the plate and the newspaper. For the first five minutes he almost had himself convinced that he could eat the potatoes and the roast beef, and read the paper as if nothing were wrong, but in the end, he couldn't do it.

He set the fork beside his plate and ran his hands down his face. He missed her. He missed her unbearably. And he understood at least part of what Hilton was saying. This loneliness really was the rest of his life. Unless he did something, he would be alone forever. But he was so damned scared to trust life, so damned afraid that life was setting him up again, that he just didn't think he could make the moves he needed to make, and say the things he needed to say, to get her back. And even if he did, it wouldn't be fair to her, because when push came to shove he would never again be able to love without reserve. And Olivia deserved to be loved without condition, wholly, completely and forever.

So he went to bed with the latest feasibility study, but without the pajamas that reminded him of Olivia being in his home. The next morning when his alarm rang, he woke with the book still open on his chest, and though he knew that was pathetic he refused to acknowledge it.

By focusing on trying to recall what he had read the night before, he showered and managed to get downstairs without thinking about her and without thinking less of himself because he was so afraid. But when he got to the bottom of his steps and was standing in his foyer, the doorbell rang.

Confused, because he had no clue who would be dropping in on him on a Thursday morning, Josh opened his front door to find his cousin Gina standing on the other side.

"Good morning."

"Good morning," Josh said, perplexed, because if she wanted to see him all she had to do was wait about an hour and they would be in the same building. She hadn't needed to drive to his house.

But before Josh could voice his questions, Gina reached behind her and produced a little girl who looked to be about six. She had blond hair, and though her eyes were a different shade of green than Olivia's, the child looked exactly how Josh expected a daughter of Olivia's would look.

"This is Renee. She's selling Girl Scout cookies, and my father insisted that I bring her to your house this morning so that you could buy some from her."

Josh swallowed. Hilton hadn't insisted that Gina bring the little girl to him so he could buy cookies, he had done it to show Josh what he was missing. Hilton knew the minute Josh looked at this little girl he would recognize that this was what Olivia's child would look like, and he wanted Josh to actually, physically see what he was giving up.

Josh stepped away from his door. "Sure. I'll buy some cookies. Come in."

"Really?" Gina said, sounding totally baffled. "You don't look much like the cookie type to me. I couldn't believe that my father was absolutely positive you would want to order, but I guess he knows you better than I do.''

''He *thinks* he knows me better than he does,'' Josh said. He filled out the form by ordering one box of each kind of cookie, if only so he wouldn't waste the poor kid's time, then he ushered them out.

Perplexed, Gina stared at him. ''I don't get it.''

''Tell your dad, I don't get it, either,'' Josh said before he closed the door on his confounded cousin.

Hilton's hitting below the belt made Josh angry, and he thought about it the entire time he drove to work. He couldn't believe that overconfident old man believed that seeing one very adorable little girl could make him melt. Because he refused to melt. He was a hell of a lot stronger than everybody gave him credit for. That was how he had survived for five years, by refusing to give up or give in to all the emotions that bombarded him all day long, every damned day.

Still, he could clearly recall the angelic features of Renee's face, and he knew that Hilton was correct about at least one thing. Olivia's daughter would look exactly like that. In fact, she might have little blond boys some day, too...

That brought him up short. In order for Olivia to have little blond children, she was going to have to marry someone. And since Josh wasn't going to marry her that meant some stranger was going to marry his woman. Some guy from the beach was going to marry her and live with her and have breakfast with her and sleep with her.

Every muscle in Josh's body froze. He genuinely believed the blood stopped pumping through his veins. He would be damned if he would sit by and do nothing and let her marry some other man, while he slept with feasibility studies, ate bacon and eggs alone for supper four nights a week, and didn't decorate for holidays. For five years he hadn't so much as put up a sprig of holly. And he was sick of eggs. He was tired of being alone. And feasibility studies weren't the fun they had once been.

Without flicking on his turn signal, Josh began skipping across the lanes of the highway, heading for the nearest exit.

He got it. He finally got what Hilton was telling him.

She wasn't going to hurt him. She was the person who had brought him back to life. But he had hurt her. And she was through taking it!

When Olivia's mother opened her door to him, Josh handed her the three-pound ball of fluff the pet store clerk had assured him was a dog.

"What's this?"

"It's a puppy. For Olivia."

"And this is supposed to make up for everything?" Karen Brady Franklin's eyes narrowed. She was the picture of Olivia with her pale yellow hair and big green-blue eyes, so she wasn't exactly frightening or imposing when she scowled at him. "Don't think I don't know who you are."

"I know you know who I am. We met at three company picnics." He paused and smiled encouragingly while the little white fuzz ball squirmed in Karen's arms. "Can I talk with Olivia?"

"All right," Mrs. Franklin said grudgingly. She turned and faced the steps behind her. "Olivia!" she called. "There's somebody here to see you." When she faced Josh again, there was fire in her eyes. "You hurt her and I will personally do something incredibly mean to you."

Because she couldn't actually say what that mean thing would be, Josh smiled. "You don't have it in you. Neither does Olivia."

"Neither do I what?" Olivia asked, walking down the steps.

"You don't have it in you to be really, really mean. Neither does your mother."

"And you drove all the way to Florida to tell us that?"

"No, I drove all the way to Florida to apologize."

By now Olivia had reached the bottom of the steps. Wearing blue jeans and a T-shirt, but no shoes, she was a good six inches shorter than he was. She looked up at him. "You should have called."

"Why? Do you have somewhere to go?"

"An interview."

"In jeans," he said skeptically.

"I've decided I'm tired of being a secretary and I'm going to try my hand at being the helper on a fishing boat."

He stared at her. "You're kidding, right?"

"Why? Don't I look strong enough or smart enough or good enough to work on a fishing boat?" she asked, crossing her arms over her chest and staring at him as if he were evil incarnate.

Josh decided she had a very good reason. He had done nothing but hurt her and now it appeared he was insulting her.

"Is there somewhere we can go to talk privately?"

"You can use the den," her mother offered, still flashing him her cautious, skeptical look.

"Can I have my dog back?"

Olivia instantly brightened. "Your dog?"

"Yeah, I bought us a dog."

"Us?"

He sighed. "Could we talk about this in the den?"

"It's back that way," Karen said, handing the squirming ball of white fur to Josh.

"*That's* your dog?" Olivia said, but she laughed. "That's not a dog. It looks like a squeezy toy for a really big cat."

"His name is Killer and he's going to grow to be the size of half our house," Josh said, directing Olivia to precede him down the hall, but she paused and took the puppy from his hands.

"You're not a Killer," she said, nuzzling his neck.

"He's going to be a Killer because he's going to protect our children from strangers. It's a wacky world out there and I don't want to take any chances with our kids."

They finished the walk to the den and Olivia turned on him. "Why are you saying these things? Why are you even here? You made it abundantly clear that you didn't want a relationship with me...or anybody, so I don't think it's fair that you—"

He stopped her tirade by grabbing her upper arms and pulling her to him to kiss her soundly. He felt all the wonderful things he felt every time he kissed her, but this time they were intensified with the knowledge that this wasn't a fluke or a mistake. These feelings weren't going away. He was in love. If he had his way he would be getting married. His life was finally back to normal.

He pulled away and took Olivia by the shoulders so he could look into her eyes and make sure she not only understood, but also believed everything he was about to tell her. "You are the best thing that ever happened to me. You kept me alive for the past four years, even though I didn't know it. But Hilton did. It's why he bribed you to stay. He knew I would die without you."

"You wouldn't have died."

"I had already eaten the last of the leftover roast beef and I wasn't yet ready to go shopping for eggs. If nothing else, I probably would have starved."

Her lips twitched.

"I drove across all five lanes of the interstate without using a turn signal."

For that, her lips lifted completely into a smile. "Oh, you do have a death wish."

"And I slept with a feasibility study last night. Two hundred pages of how Bee-Great Groceries plans to steal our market share were sprawled across my chest. Instead of a blanket...instead of a woman...instead of you. I want you."

Suddenly, and unexpectedly, Olivia threw her arms around his neck. She clung to him and began to cry. "Oh, Josh, I've been so worried about you."

"I've been a little worried about myself, too, until I realized that I didn't want you sleeping with anybody else, making babies with anybody else. And I got jealous, but not in a way that was nuts and crazy. In my head I said something like I'm not going to sit back and let that happen, and then I knew."

She pushed away far enough that she could see his face. "Knew what?"

"Knew that I loved you and I wasn't going to drag you down by pulling you into a relationship with somebody who couldn't handle it. I could handle it. I would have fought the devil for you."

She grimaced. "Let's hope it doesn't go that far."

"How far do you want it to go?"

"I want to get married, I want to have kids...I want to keep the dog, but you can't name him Killer. I want him to be Ringo or Rusty or Champ."

"Ringo?"

"What? Rusty or Champ is fine, but there's something inherently wrong with Ringo?"

"It's not really a dog's name."

"Well, it's not really a good name for the drummer of a rock band, but Ringo Starr did okay."

"All right, I'm not going to argue with you," Josh said, feeling a love so strong and so deep he wondered how he had lived this long without noticing it had been around him for four entire years. "You can name him Ringo Starr if you want."

"Star... Maybe we'll just name him Star...or Sunshine...or Ralph."

"Are you going to have this much trouble naming our kids?"

"Why? Would that make you change your mind about me?"

For that he smiled. The reaction was so quick and spontaneous that he knew it was a permanent phenomenon. "Nothing is going to make me change my mind about how I feel about you."

"Good, because nothing is ever going to change my mind about how I feel about you."

"Thank God, because I love you," he said, and kissed her again. But another thought struck him and he pulled away. "Hey, we could sleep together tonight...."

"Not on your life."

"No?"

"You haven't bought me flowers or candy or even

taken me to a movie. First things first, bud. You owe me. You owe me big time."

"I know," he agreed, then started to laugh. "I owe you big time."

He pulled her to him and kissed her again, feeling joy—real joy—pouring back into his life, and he knew he did owe her. He knew he owed her big time. But he also knew he would spend the rest of his life blissfully repaying his debt to her.

*   *   *   *   *

Award-winning author
SHARON DE VITA
brings her special brand of romance to

Silhouette

SPECIAL EDITION™
and

SILHOUETTE *Romance*™

in her new cross-line miniseries

SADDLE FALLS

This small Western town was rocked by scandal when the youngest son of the prominent Ryan family was kidnapped. Watch as clues about the mysterious disappearance are unveiled—and meet the sexy Ryan brothers...along with the women destined to lasso their hearts.

Don't miss:

WITH FAMILY IN MIND
February 2002, Silhouette Special Edition #1450

ANYTHING FOR HER FAMILY
March 2002, Silhouette Romance #1580

A FAMILY TO BE
April 2002, Silhouette Romance #1586

A FAMILY TO COME HOME TO
May 2002, Silhouette Special Edition #1468

Available at your favorite retail outlet.

Silhouette®
Where love comes alive™

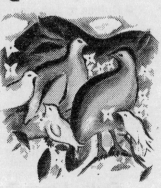

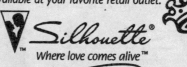